THE FORTUNES OF TEXAS

*Follow the lives and loves of a complex family
with a rich history and deep ties
in the Lone Star State*

FORTUNE'S HIDDEN TREASURES

A new branch of the Fortune family heads to idyllic
Emerald Ridge to solve a decades-long mystery
that died with their parents, and a mysterious loss
that upends their lives. Little do they know that
their hearts will never be the same!

FORTUNE FOR A WEEK

Sofia Gomez Simon can't believe that one
impulsive night in Vegas left her with a ring on her
finger and Emerald Ridge's most eligible bachelor
as her husband! Harris Fortune can marshal all his
considerable resources to end the marriage...but
after he plays house with Sofia and her adorable
kids, maybe neither of them wants to!

Dear Reader,

Family is everything to me. That's one of the reasons I love writing books in the Fortunes of Texas series. The Fortunes are a vast and eclectic bunch. Yet the one thing they have in common is that family always comes first.

Harris Fortune, the hero of my book, lost both of his parents at a tender age. Even though his cousin, Sander, who was barely of age himself, graciously raised Harris and his siblings, Harris has always longed for a traditional family of his own. When he meets single mother Sofia Gomez Simon and her two children, he believes he has met the woman—and family—of his dreams. When an unexpected Vegas marriage throws their life into chaos, Harris is all in, but Sofia isn't sure the surprise marriage is the best thing for her children. Will ten days of family life with Harris unlock her guarded heart?

I hope you'll love Harris and Sofia's story as much as I enjoyed writing it. Please let me know what you think. You can connect with me through my website, nancyrobardsthompson.com, on Facebook at Facebook.com/nrobardsthompson and Instagram at Instagram.com/nancyrthompson.

xoxo,

Nancy

FORTUNE FOR A WEEK

NANCY ROBARDS THOMPSON

THE FORTUNES OF TEXAS

Special thanks and acknowledgment are given to Nancy Robards Thompson for her contribution to The Fortunes of Texas: Fortune's Hidden Treasures miniseries.

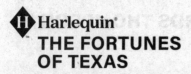

Harlequin
THE FORTUNES OF TEXAS

Recycling programs for this product may not exist in your area.

ISBN-13: 978-1-335-14327-3

Fortune for a Week

Harlequin Enterprises ULC
22 Adelaide St. West, 41st Floor
Toronto, Ontario M5H 4E3, Canada
www.Harlequin.com

Printed in Lithuania

MIX
Paper | Supporting responsible forestry
FSC® C021394

USA TODAY bestselling author **Nancy Robards Thompson** has a degree in journalism. She worked as a newspaper reporter until she realized reporting "just the facts" was boring. Happier to report to her muse, Nancy has found Nirvana writing women's fiction, romance and cozy mysteries full-time. Critics have deemed her work "funny, smart and observant." She lives in Tennessee with her husband and their corgi. For more, please visit her website at nancyrobardsthompson.com.

Books by Nancy Robards Thompson

Harlequin Special Edition

The McFaddens of Tinsley Cove

Selling Sandcastle
Rules of Engagement

The Savannah Sisters

A Down-Home Savannah Christmas
Southern Charm & Second Chances
Her Savannah Surprise

Celebration, TX

The Cowboy's Runaway Bride
A Bride, a Barn, and a Baby
The Cowboy Who Got Away

The Fortunes of Texas: Rambling Rose

Betting on a Fortune

The Fortunes of Texas: Digging for Secrets

Worth a Fortune

The Fortunes of Texas: Fortune's Hidden Treasures

Fortune for a Week

Visit the Author Profile page
at Harlequin.com for more titles.

This book is dedicated to Susan Litman for all you do.
The Fortunes wouldn't be what it is without you.

Chapter One

Maybe it was the scantily-clad women juggling bottles of *Circo Lujoso* hair dye or the fact that *Circo Lujoso* translated to *luxurious circus*, but the words *There's a sucker born every minute* echoed in Harris Fortune's mind.

"This is a ground-floor opportunity…don't miss out!" shouted the guy who was dressed in the red coat of a ringmaster. Alejandro…something or the other.

Harris glanced at the prospectus he'd picked up when he'd entered the meeting room.

Garces.

Alejandro Garces. His résumé touted that this colorist to the stars had developed *Circo Lujoso*'s unique formula after working with substandard brands for more than two decades. Now, he was seeking investors.

"Just as people all over the world wish Alejandro Garces, the king of color, would lay his magic hands on their hair, investors from around the world will covet the chance to invest in this amazing early-stage opportunity. Alejandro Garces has selected you."

And now he was referring to himself in the third person.

Nope. This is not for me.

The invitation had arrived yesterday, which hadn't allowed much time for his staff to perform due diligence. Now, he had to wonder if the timing of the invite signaled that others had turned down the opportunity.

If Harris hadn't already been in Las Vegas for another meeting, he wouldn't be here right now. But he *was* here and the buzz around the product had lured him in. However, after listening to the hype, something beyond the fact that hair dye didn't fit in with the rest of the investments in his portfolio wasn't sitting right with him.

The music flared again and blasted another circus tune. Harris stood to leave.

He'd heard enough. This investment—and this spectacle of a circus—wasn't for him.

He'd turned down his fair share of investment opportunities, but this hair dye presentation was easily the most ridiculous of his career: a hair color formulation from Spain that supposedly took a year to fade and was not only the talk of the convention but apparently an international sensation.

For that matter, he used to love Vegas, but this time, it felt like a drag. Maybe at thirty-two he was finally over it.

"Remember, you must be present to win the opportunity to experience the magic of *Circo Lujoso*," Garces called.

Sensing someone behind him as he opened the door to leave the meeting room, Harris glanced back.

An attractive brunette was ten paces behind him. He held the door to let her exit first.

"Thanks," she said as she ducked out and the door closed behind them.

"So, you weren't sold either?" he asked.

She laughed and shook her head.

"I'm sorry. I don't care if he is the legendary Alejandro Garces. No hair color in the world, not even a formula from the most magical place, will last a year without fading. I've been in the business a long time, and I can tell you that with confidence."

The strangest sense of déjà vu gripped Harris.

He held out his hand. "I'm Harris Fortune. Have we met? You look familiar."

"Sofia Gomez Simon." Her hand was soft, but her grip was confident. "I own The Style Lounge salon in Emerald Ridge."

"Texas?"

Surprise flashed in her lovely brown eyes. "Yes. Have you heard of it?"

"I have. My family…" He weighed his words as it dawned on him where he'd seen Sofia before. "We have ties to Emerald Ridge."

A few years ago, when he was at his family's compound in the well-to-do small town, he'd noticed her as he'd thumbed through an issue of *Emerald*, the local magazine that kept a finger on the town's business and cultural heartbeat. Successful salon owner Sofia Simon Gomez had been featured in an article spotlighting the town's top five most successful businesswomen.

He couldn't remember the details of the article, and her hair was different now, but he'd never forget that face.

"Small world." She narrowed her eyes. "You're not planning on opening a salon there, are you? Because I'll warn you up front that all the best stylists in town work for me, and my clients are faithful."

"Are they?" he said.

She nodded. He liked the confident tilt of her head and the way her eyes held his gaze. Given her conviction, even if he were keen on opening a competing salon, he wouldn't want to try to wrestle any of those faithful clients away from her.

On second thought, it might be kind of fun to wrestle with her and get his hands on those enticing curves.

"I'm serious," she reiterated. "Emerald Ridge is a small town and its population wouldn't support two high-end salons. And as I said, my clients are faithful."

"Faithfulness is important to you," he said.

She blinked and gave a barely perceptible shake of her head. Not a shake that denied his statement; it was more like the idea had caught her by surprise.

The uncertainty faded fast. She checked her posture and pulled herself up to her full height of...well, she was wearing sexy stiletto heels with that curve-hugging blue dress, but he'd guess, in her bare feet, she couldn't have been more than five-two.

"I do appreciate faithfulness," she murmured. "When a person is true to their word—honors commitments—it says a lot about who they are."

He nodded. That was interesting. The vulnerable note in her voice made the situation sound personal.

"I agree," he said. "Keeping promises is important."

Discreetly, his gaze fell to her left ring finger and found it enticingly bare.

Suddenly, he felt reenergized. Maybe this trip wouldn't turn out to be such a waste after all.

"I am starving," he said. "Want to grab a bite to eat? There's a new restaurant on Freemont Street that I'm dying to try. They have a wonderful tasting menu with wine pairings."

When she hesitated, he added, "Just one Emerald Ridge resident having supper with another."

Harris Fortune had just asked her to dinner.

The split second after he'd introduced himself, she'd realized who he was...this was Harris frickin' Fortune.

Then it had taken only another split second for her to rein in the ridiculous giddiness spawned by his invitation.

Even though the offer was enticing and she was famished—she'd been too busy to eat anything since the coffee and muffin she'd had for breakfast—she couldn't go to dinner with him.

Her divorce had only been final for three months. Of course, she and her ex-husband, Dan, had been separated for a while before the decree dissolving their marriage landed. The concept that she was *divorced* was still so bizarre that she flinched inwardly every time she referred to Dan as her *ex*.

That in itself should've been proof that she wasn't in the headspace to date. But no, there was another reason she'd sworn off dating: her children. Kaitlin Maria was only seven and Jackson Carlos was a year younger.

She and Dan had upended their young lives when they'd mutually agreed they were better friends than husband and wife, and a broken home was healthier for their children than one in which their parents were constantly fighting.

The ultimate litmus test was that even now when she dissected the situation, she still believed that ending the marriage was the right thing to do.

Sure, she had regrets. But their decision to divorce wasn't one of them.

Even so, she wouldn't be dating for a long time. Probably not until the kids were in college.

"I appreciate the offer," she said. "I'm leaving tomorrow. So I need to pack and get myself together."

She started to walk away but turned around and smiled.

"I'm serious now. Emerald Ridge is not big enough for two salons. The Style Lounge rivals any salon you'd find in Dallas. If you don't believe me, just make an appointment and let me prove it to you."

She did that thing where she pursed her lips and smoldered through her eyes. Dan used to call it her Marilyn Monroe *kiss me if you can* face…even though she looked nothing like Marilyn Monroe—

Stop it, Sofia. What in the world do you think you're doing? Flirting, that's what. With Harris Fortune.

Well, stop it. Just walk away.

His brows lifted, but she turned before he could say anything.

Her heart was thudding from the adrenaline rush, and when her text tone sounded, indicating a new message, she jumped a little. Like she'd been caught doing something she shouldn't.

She expected to see a message from one of her kids. Dan had come up to Emerald Ridge from Austin to stay with them at the house while she was at the convention. He'd been letting them text her from his phone several times a day.

She frowned when she saw it was from her cousin Jacinta.

The preview said: WTF?

Sofia stopped and opened the text, which contained a photo of Dan. A pretty brunette was sitting on his lap with her arms around his neck. They weren't kissing, but their noses were together as if they were about to or just had—

Why was Jacinta sending this to her?

Underneath the picture, her cousin had texted: Did you know about this????

Of course not. How would she have known about it? It's not as if Dan or whoever had snapped the photo would've sent it to her. And why did Jacinta have it?

Was she trying to twist the knife, rubbing Sofia's nose in the fact that not only had Jacinta inherited their abuela Rosa's chocolate business, but that she'd also landed herself a man in the process?

A Fortune man, at that.

Jacinta was married to Micah Fortune.

And Sofia was a thirty-year-old divorced mother of two.

She loved her cousin. Really, she did, but she wouldn't be telling the truth if she didn't acknowledge that they had a knack for pushing each other's buttons.

Sofia rolled her eyes and considered how to reply.

Actually, she didn't mind that Jacinta had taken over their abuela's chocolate business and had found love. Good for her. *Go, Jacinta.* Sofia had her own thriving business in the salon. She hadn't wanted to make chocolate anyway.

But what she *did* mind was that Jacinta seemed to take pleasure in passive-aggressively rubbing her nose in the fact that Sofia and Dan were…divorced.

She studied the photo again as her thumbs danced over her phone's keyboard.

Dan is free to play kissy-face with anyone he wants…especially when the brunette looks a lot like me— He definitely has a type.

Then she backspaced over the message, deleting it as fast as she'd created it.

As she considered an alternate reply, Harris Fortune walked by and smiled at her.

"Hey, Harris," she said. "I've changed my mind. I'd love to have dinner with you. If your offer still stands."

What was a meal between friends? Albeit two *new* friends.

They were in Vegas, after all. It's not as if her kids or anyone else from Emerald Ridge would see them together and get the wrong idea. Or take a picture of her sitting on his lap.

There would be *no* sitting on his lap, she reminded herself sharply, because it was just two Emerald Ridge residents having dinner together.

* * *

Harris touched his wineglass to Sofia's.

She took a sip and said, "You never answered my question. Are you opening a salon? In Emerald Ridge or anywhere else?"

He considered making her wonder a bit longer because competition seemed to bring out her fierce side, but the evening was off to such a good start. They were sitting at a cozy corner table in Laurel, a brand-new restaurant that had a three-month waiting list for reservations. The wait was even longer for a Saturday night. Harris had gone to college with one of the owners, who had invited him when he'd learned he'd be in town tonight.

They were enjoying the first offering of a six-course tasting menu, complete with wine pairings.

"Salons aren't exactly my brand." He speared a bite of his grilled asparagus, put it in his mouth and chewed.

"If you're not opening a salon or investing in one, why are you at a hair trade show in Las Vegas?" Sofia asked curiously.

"I received an invitation to attend the *Circo Lujoso* showcase. I happened to be in town for another meeting, and I decided to see if all the hype surrounding the hair dye was true."

"Ah, okay," she said. "And here we are."

"And here we are. Were you lured to Vegas by Garces's investment opportunity?"

"No. I come to this trade show to learn about new products and keep up with what's new in the industry. I wasn't invited to the meeting." She offered a sheepish shrug. "I just walked in."

Her embarrassment was short-lived. "Naturally, I was curious to learn about the product. I may not be in a position to invest, but I *am* a salon owner. It's people like me who will buy the product and keep Garces's circus running."

"Will you use it if it hits the market?"

She grimaced. "I don't mislead my clients, and no hair color will last a year without fading. It's nonsense to create buzz around that. But let's say it did last a year—a client will have a natural grow-out, which means they will still have to come in for touch-ups. The other thing that worries me is that he isn't forthcoming with the ingredients. I don't want to expose my clients to caustic chemicals or have my hands in them. I just don't understand where Garces is going with it. These days, the trend seems to be moving more toward natural colors and treatments anyway."

The server approached the table with two more glasses of wine. "Mr. Woodward asked me to send these over to you. It's a new vintage that's not usually served with this course, but he would love your opinions. Is everything alright with your plate, ma'am?"

Sofia glanced down at her untouched asparagus as if noticing it for the first time. "Everything's fine." She smiled at Harris. "I've just been talking too much."

She picked up her knife and fork and cut a piece.

"Tell Carl thank you for the wine," Harris said.

With a quick nod, the server left them alone.

"I've been talking too much," Sofia confessed. "I apologize. I'm passionate about what I do and sometimes I have to rein myself in. Plus, I wanted to tell you why I snuck into that meeting uninvited."

He loved her passion.

"It wasn't as if you crashed the gate."

She smiled. "Gate-crashing definitely isn't my style."

"Even if it was, I like your style, Sofia Gomez Simon." Harris raised his wineglass to hers.

Her cheeks colored and she took another sip.

"Do you mind if I ask you a question?" he asked.

"Ask me anything," she said and sipped again.

"Your last name is Gomez Simon. Are you related to Jacinta Gomez? She's married to my cousin Micah."

"Yes, Jacinta is my cousin. I figured all you Fortunes are related somehow."

Harris laughed. "I think we are. But a more important question is, since your cousin is married to my cousin, does that make us related somehow?"

"Maybe cousins-in-law?" Her eyes glinted. "Not in a way that matters."

A hint of innuendo hung between them. If this had been any other woman, he would've called her double entendre and raised the stakes until they decided to ditch dinner and go straight to dessert…in her hotel room.

Instead, instinct told him to take this slowly. "Where does the Simon part of your name come from?"

She seemed to flinch. It was barely perceptible, but he saw it.

Then she drew her lips between her teeth and stared down at her hands before exhaling and looking him square in the eyes.

"I was married. Not anymore."

The relief that flooded through Harris made him feel like a kid who'd awakened on Christmas morning to discover Santa had left him exactly what he'd wanted. But he was determined not to let it show because she didn't seem thrilled.

It was divorce, after all, and it stood to reason she wouldn't be happy about it.

"How long has it been?" he asked softly.

The uncomfortable look that had transformed her pretty face earlier when she'd been talking about sneaking into the *Circo Lujoso* hair dye prospectus meeting returned.

She drained the rest of her wine.

"The divorce has been final for three months, but we were separated for a while before we filed. Honestly, the relationship had been over for a lot longer than that. I'm sorry. You don't want to hear about that. I've monopolized the conversation tonight. Please tell me about you."

"If I didn't want to hear about it, I wouldn't have asked. Are you…" He set down his wineglass and raked his hand over his face. "How do I put this…?"

She tilted her head to the side and a slight smile tilted up the corners of her luscious mouth. Suddenly, tasting her lips was the only thing he was craving.

"What?" She leaned forward. "Just say it."

Their gazes snared and something passed between them.

"I guess what I'm trying to ask is, are you still hung up on your ex-husband?"

Her eyes widened, but there was a glint in them that hinted that she wasn't offended by the question.

"Dan and I got married way too young—before we really knew ourselves or realized there was a big, wide world out there beyond Emerald Ridge. We were high school sweethearts. You know, it was a first love thing—and before we knew it, eight years had passed and we had two kids. But we barely knew each other…"

She shrugged and pushed her plate away just in time for the server to approach with their second course and more wine.

As the server poured lobster bisque from something that looked like a gravy boat into white china bowls, Harris didn't hear what the man said because his mind wandered. Sofia hadn't answered his question about whether she was still in love with—or hung up on—her ex.

He shouldn't have asked. The divorce had only been final a few months and they had kids. That little tidbit had just wormed its way through the wine haze that had been shrouding his rational thinking.

This woman had a lot of baggage. He just needed to leave it alone.

And just treat this as a dinner between two new acquaintances who shared the same hometown and had bumped into each other out of town. Away from prying eyes and ex-husbands and children—

"Sir?" the server said.

"Yes?" Harris answered, and noticed the long pepper grinder the server was offering.

"Pepper on your bisque?"

"Yes, please."

"Now, our sommelier will explain the wine she and chef have paired with this course."

The server stepped back and the sommelier began. "This evening, we've chosen an Italian rosé to accompany your lobster bisque. It's made with Sangiovese grapes, which are one of Italy's top varieties. Surprisingly, they are rarely used in rosés, which is a shame because they create a nice, balanced wine. This might be an unexpected choice, but it works well because the hint of fruit remains dry and complements the delicacy of the lobster without overpowering it. Enjoy."

"Thank you," Harris said. While he would never be rude to someone who was just doing her job, he'd had to fight the urge to dismiss her before the moment with Sofia was gone. If it wasn't already.

After the sommelier stepped away, Harris took the time to lift his glass once again to Sofia.

"Santé."

After they'd tasted the soup and raved about its deliciousness, he said, "Where did we leave off?"

She shrugged, and he studied her face for signs of whether or not he should push her to continue the conversation.

But he wanted to know more about her, so he nudged. "Eight years had passed. You and Dan had two kids, but you barely knew each other…"

She smiled. "You're a good listener, but are you sure you want to hear this?"

He swallowed his bite and sat back in his chair, giving her his full attention. "I'm all ears."

"First, I do need to mention that you might know my ex-husband, Dan Simon. He used to work for Micah Fortune at Fortune's Gold Ranch."

"I've never met your ex. I don't spend much time at the Fortune ranch, to be honest."

Sofia arched a brow. "Really?"

He shrugged. "I live in Dallas. I don't have anything to do with the ranch. It belongs to my cousin. When I come to Emerald Ridge, it's mostly for relaxation or family get-togethers."

She studied him for a moment and he couldn't read what she might be thinking.

"So, you don't really live in Emerald Ridge, then?"

Harris was on to her. He was not going to let her steer this conversation away from herself. She still hadn't answered his question.

"If I said no, would it be a good thing or a bad thing?"

She leaned in again, her forearms resting on the table. Her eyes were bright, and the wine had brought out the color on her cheeks.

"I don't know. You tell me, Harris. Would not living in Emerald Ridge be a good or bad thing?"

"I guess that depends on whether you still have feelings for your ex."

She glanced at her hands again. Was she looking at where

her wedding band had been—or was he imagining it? Whatever the case, she sat back in her chair.

Dammit. The spell was broken. Clearly, there was something still between her and Dan and, if he had to guess, it was
more than the two children they shared.

"It's complicated," she admitted. "I do still love my
husband—er ex-husband, but not in a romantic way. I will
always care for him deeply. I mean, he's the father of my babies, and I want them always to have a good relationship with
their dad. I still have a good relationship with their father,
but that's the crux of the matter. Dan and I are better friends
than lovers. Or, um, what I mean is that we're better at being
friends than being married."

She punctuated the words with a quick lift and release of
the shoulders, then added, "Do you think I could have another glass of rosé? I really like it."

Harris caught their server's eye and then held up his glass,
signaling he'd like two more glasses.

Soon, Carl Woodward returned with a tray containing five
glasses of wine and a bottle.

"Hello," he said. "I've been meaning to get over here before now, but we've been slammed tonight."

Carl put the wine on the table, reserving one glass for himself right before another member of the wait staff whisked
away the tray in a seamless move that almost seemed cho-
reographed.

"I'm glad to see business is going so well." Harris and Carl
shook hands. "Thank you for getting us in tonight. Carl, this
is my friend, Sofia Gomez Simon. Sofia, this is Carl Woodward. Carl and I go way back. We went to college together,
and now he's a world-class restaurateur."

"Nice to meet you, Carl. Everything is delicious."

They made small talk for a moment, and the man explained

that the extra glasses of wine he'd brought over was a rosé from another vineyard, this one French.

He set it in front of Sofia. "Which one do you prefer?"

Harris and Carl watched her as she took her time swirling, sniffing and tasting each of the wines.

"I think I prefer the Italian," she answered.

"Good, I'll leave the bottle," Carl said as he refilled their glasses.

A warmth expanded inside Harris as he watched her subtly lick the wine from her lips. He was craving a taste of those lips. Instinctively, he knew they would be more delicious than anything he'd tasted tonight…maybe more than anything he'd tasted in his life.

And that was the wine talking.

Maybe.

He'd felt an attraction to her when he'd been stone-cold sober this afternoon. Hell, he'd been attracted to her years ago when he'd first seen her in that magazine.

He was at war with himself.

Part of him wanted to say, *This is Vegas, baby. What happens here stays between you and me.*

But another more sensible voice of reason—the one that was slowly but surely being drowned out by the alcohol and the magnetic pull of her—warned him that he was playing with fire if he fooled around with a woman like that so soon after her divorce.

A woman with two kids… A woman who lived in Emerald Ridge, a place that was once his retreat but had already been tainted by his old friend Linc Banning's murder.

Even from the little bit he knew about the case, Harris could see that during the five years since he and Linc had been in touch, his friend had gotten mixed up in something shady. Yet law enforcement didn't seem overly motivated to get to the bottom of it. That was one of the reasons he'd decided to stay in Emerald Ridge for a while. To see what he could find out and help move the case along.

Well, that and this scavenger hunt that his late parents had inadvertently left for his siblings and him. They were all trying to locate this "surprise" their mom and dad had supposedly left them before they'd died.

Harris blew out a breath. He had enough on his plate without having to worry about running into his Vegas conquest around every corner in Emerald Ridge. And the truth of the matter was a woman like Sofia Gomez Simon deserved to be more than a Vegas conquest.

Right now, he didn't have it in him.

"Hey, it was good to see you, man." Carl slapped Harris on the back. "Let me know the next time you two are in town and I'll reserve a table for you."

He didn't try to explain that there probably wouldn't be a next time. He simply thanked Carl for the hospitality.

"So, I have a question for you," Sofia said after Carl walked away.

"Okay, shoot," Harris said.

"Do you believe in love?"

"What? As in the Cher song?"

"No, that's life after love," she said. "I'm serious. Do you believe in love that lasts forever? That two people can meet and fall in love and stay together for the rest of their lives?"

Chapter Two

Sofia couldn't believe the words that were falling out of her mouth like those colorful fruity candies in that television commercial about chasing a rainbow. Or maybe it was tasting a rainbow. She couldn't remember. All she knew for sure was that she couldn't stop the words.

But maybe that wasn't such a bad thing.

Perhaps she was more ready to talk about her failed marriage than she thought.

Harris was looking at her thoughtfully, and a warmth started in the most private of private places…a place from which she thought she'd been permanently disconnected because it wouldn't get any action for a very long time.

Nope. She was feeling it. An itch that needed to be scratched and was all but demanding that she let Harris Fortune do the honors.

And that was so *not* happening.

But, man, oh man, was he gorgeous.

She shifted in her seat and sighed inwardly as she tried to focus her attention on all that thick blond hair. How she'd love to get her hands in it.

Hmm…did he have a stylist in Emerald Ridge?

"I do," he said.

Sofia blinked. "You do? Wait, what?"

Had he read her mind? She knew that was ridiculous. Maybe she'd said the words out loud?

She'd had a lot of wine tonight. Way too much. Yep. She was a little tipsy.

Okay, more than a little tipsy. She was drunk.

She would woman-up and admit it.

She was DRUNK. She'd paused between the N and K to double-check that she wasn't shouting it to the restaurant.

Nope. She was good. She could *landle* her *hicker*. Er, wine. She needed coffee, but according to the cute little menu the server had given them, the coffee was the last course.

They were still four courses away. What she needed to do was eat. Get something in her stomach.

As she was spooning a bite of lobster bisque into her mouth, Harris said, "You asked me if I believed in love."

Luckily, she'd swallowed the soup before he'd said that because she might've choked on it.

Come on, Sofia. Don't embarrass yourself.

"You do?" She set her spoon down. "You believe in love."

"Yeah, why not?" he said. "Don't you?"

She shook her head. "He asks this of a woman who's been divorced for three months after ending an eight-year marriage."

He nodded, confirming that she had, indeed, said that part out loud.

"So you seriously don't believe in love?" he prodded.

"No, I don't. Not anymore."

He pushed his empty bowl back, braced his elbow on the table and rested his chin on his fist.

"That's so sad," he said. "A beautiful woman like you should be surrounded by love."

"I am," she said. "In a way. My children love me. I have a fabulous family. See, I have all the love I need."

She grinned, but his face looked way too serious. It sobered her a bit.

"What?" she said.

"Dan Simon must've done a number on you to make you give up on love."

His words touched a tender spot in her heart. It felt like he was poking at a bruise.

Once, she had cared deeply for Dan, but the two of them had fallen out of love—the feeling had been mutual—and while she was no longer into her ex-husband, the split still hurt. Because, once upon a time, it was supposed to be forever and it didn't last.

She shook her head and then shrugged halfheartedly.

"I can't let Dan shoulder all the blame. A marriage takes two people. He's a decent guy. He even built a little casita in our backyard so that I could start my business there. That way, I didn't have to work for anyone else or deal with any of the BS that sometimes goes on in a salon. Now, I have a great guesthouse in the backyard that sits empty because I'm so busy that I never have time to host anyone."

She toyed with her spoon, moving it back and forth, getting lost in her thoughts for a moment. Then she put her hands in her lap and looked Harris straight in the eyes.

"My ex is also a fabulous father and a good friend. Or at least I think he will be. Someday. After the bruises heal."

Harris stiffened. "Bruises? Did he hurt you? I mean physically."

"No! I wasn't speaking in the literal sense. Breakups are hard, even when they are mutual. They leave behind figurative bruises. Think about it. There was a time in our lives when we took a vow to love each other for the rest of our lives. But Dan and I couldn't do it. Not even for the sake of the kids. The whole experience left me with the realization that maybe human beings weren't meant to pledge themselves to one person forever."

She started to add, *Because if it had been possible to do that, Dan and I would still be together.* But then she remembered the photo that Jacinta had sent and suddenly she didn't feel quite so sentimental.

Dan was moving on. If he could do that so easily, maybe she could allow herself to have some fun—at least tonight while she was in Sin City.

"Anytime you care for someone…anytime you let someone in, you make yourself vulnerable to being hurt. It doesn't always have to be romantic love."

He frowned and something that resembled deep sadness flickered in his eyes.

"I opened up to you," she said. "Now, it's your turn."

"What's there to say?" He shrugged as if he expected her to be fine with that, but if he wanted her to pry it out of him, then she could do that, too.

She picked up her wineglass, swirled its contents, and sat back in her chair. "I have all evening. So, take your time."

She wasn't going to let him off the hook.

He nodded, picked up the wine bottle and refilled their glasses.

"Did you know Linc Banning?" he asked.

"The name sounds familiar," Sofia said, but she couldn't pull the reason why from the fuzzy recesses of her mind.

Harris took a deep breath and let it out in a slow, measured exhale.

"You might've read about him in the paper. The authorities recently found his body in the river."

Sofia gasped. "Yes, I did read about it. Did you know him?"

Harris nodded. "Linc and I were best buds as kids. Now he's gone. Someone murdered him."

She reached over and touched his hand. "Oh no, Harris, that's so awful. You're right…it's not only romantic love that can break your heart. Do they have any idea who killed him?"

He shrugged. "The authorities say they're working on the case."

They sat in silence for a moment and Sofia racked her brain for something to say. She and Dan had mutually agreed to divorce, but what did you say to someone who'd had a person they cared about brutally ripped away from them?

"I'm really sorry" was all she could come up with.

"Thanks. Linc and I had lost touch over the years, but when we were growing up, he'd been like part of the family. His mom used to work for us, and one day, out of the blue, he said something about how we couldn't be friends because he was the housekeeper's kid and I was…" Harris shrugged again. "I told him that none of that mattered, but one day, he started acting like a different person. It was like he didn't want to know me anymore.

"Funny thing is, I just learned that my sister Priscilla not only had reconnected with him, but the two of them had secretly dated. Linc even left her his houseboat. So go figure."

"I really hope they catch the person who did it."

"Yeah. Apparently, Linc had gotten tangled up with some shady people, and whatever he was involved in might have gotten him killed. All I know is that his death has left my entire family reeling. We're all unsettled and sad. We all loved him like a brother."

Sofia nodded.

"So there you go," Harris said. "To me, that's proof positive that love exists."

She squinted at him and he held her gaze. She forced herself not to squirm under his scrutiny.

"I don't know," she said. "We may have to agree to disagree. There's a difference between romantic love and the kind you are describing." She flashed him a winsome smile. "But in any event, we're in Vegas, Fortune. All that sad stuff will be waiting for us back in Emerald Ridge. Not to make light of your friend's death, but you know what I want to do tonight?"

He leaned in, planting his elbows on the table and clasping his hands. "What would you like to do?"

"After dinner, I want to go dancing. Will you take me dancing, Harris?"

A grin spread over his handsome face. "Your wish is my command."

After they finished dining, Harris's driver picked them up outside the restaurant.

"Where are we going?" Sofia asked as the driver steered the sleek sedan onto the highway.

"You said you wanted to dance," Harris said. "Gem Club at the Celestial Palace is one of the best nightclubs in Vegas. Does that sound alright?"

"That sounds *perfect*." Sofia sighed and settled in for the ride.

A few moments later, the car turned onto the Strip and then glided up the long drive leading to the Celestial Palace Hotel and Casino, its engine purring softly before the driver stopped under the portico. A uniformed valet opened the door and Sofia stepped out onto the polished granite driveway. The night air was warm, but a gentle breeze carried the hum of the city, mingling with the soft strains of music and people talking and laughing.

Sofia stared at the building's silver lights for a moment. "This is beautiful."

The exterior of the Celestial Palace was nothing short of spectacular. Towering glass and steel rose high into the night sky, reflecting the myriad lights of the Strip. The building was adorned with intricate, celestial-themed designs etched into the glass, illuminated by subtle, embedded lights that gave the entire structure a shimmering, otherworldly glow.

Sofia glanced around, taking in the opulence. To her left, a grand fountain dominated the circular driveway—its jets of water lit from beneath by multicolored lights, creating a mesmerizing display that danced in time with the ambient music. Surrounding the fountain were meticulously landscaped gardens, lush and vibrant, providing a striking contrast to the modernity of the hotel and the Strip's casual, touristy vibe.

"Shall we?" Harris asked as he appeared at her side and offered an arm.

Smiling giddily, she gladly accepted it.

As they approached the hotel, a doorman in a crisp, navy uniform stepped forward, offering a warm, professional smile as he opened the glass doors leading into the lobby.

"Welcome to the Celestial Palace," he said, his voice carrying a hint of practiced elegance.

She felt like she was walking on a wine-infused cloud as they entered the vast hotel and stepped into the lobby, which was a vision of luxury with marble floors, high ceilings adorned with sparkling chandeliers and walls lined with more celestial motifs. She took in the soft murmur of conversations, the clinking of glasses from the nearby bar and the distant sounds of slot machines. It was almost sensory overload.

"Gem is this way," Harris said, putting a gentle hand on the small of her back. His touch made her shiver.

Then, the thumping base of Gem nightclub pulled them in. When they got inside, the techno music seamlessly transitioned into a dance version of the Cher song, "Believe."

Sofia did a double take. "Did you plan this?" she asked over the music.

"Plan what?" Harris asked.

She made circles with her hands, meant to convey the music. Harris cocked his head to one side.

"I wish I could take credit for this place, but you said you wanted to dance, and this is the best place in Vegas."

"But the song," Sofia said. "We were talking about it at dinner, and we walk in and it starts playing. Did you call ahead?"

He squinted and smiled. "All I know is we'd better dance before it's over."

Harris took her hand and pulled her out onto the dance floor into the sea of revelers who were moving with abandon with their arms over their heads, lost in the anthem about believing in a better life after being burned by love.

She closed her eyes and let the music drift through her, moving her body as she let all of her cares go.

Funny, before tonight, the words to this song had made her tear up—the part about not being strong enough—but right now, in *this* moment, the part about moving on and knowing that she was strong stood out. The picture of that woman sitting on Dan's lap that Jacinta had sent her cauterized the wounds she'd thought would never heal.

Now, Sofia realized it was time for her to move on, too.

She opened her eyes and saw Harris dancing in front of her, watching her with an expression that looked like he didn't hate what he saw. She took his hands and he twirled her around so that the skirt of her dress fanned out. Then he lowered his arm until it rested on her shoulders.

Sofia scooted in, and he pulled her close, holding her just long enough for her to get a feel for how their bodies fit together.

And it was nice.

So nice.

Too nice.

She grabbed his hand and twirled out and away from him, giving him a look meant to suggest, *Hold that thought, but right now, I want to dance.*

And that's what they did. They danced and danced until Sofia had no idea how long they'd been out there, but she suddenly realized she was parched.

She leaned in and said, "I need something to drink."

He nodded and led her off the dance floor.

They were about halfway through their cocktails when a woman in a white-sequined minidress and shoulder-length bridal veil and a guy in a tuxedo T-shirt and black pants walked up to Sofia and Harris and held out a bottle.

At first, she wasn't sure what they were doing when the bride turned the sealed bottle of bubbly toward Sofia. Was this a new way to push bottle service?

"We just got married!" she shouted over the thumping of the music.

"Congratulations," Sofia and Harris said in unison.

"We have to get to the airport because our plane leaves in, like, two hours," the woman explained. "We won't have time to drink it. You two are such a cute couple. We want you to have it."

Sofia turned the green bottle so that she could see its yellow label. She'd expected it to be Veuve Clicquot, but she saw that it bore a custom label: Congratulations from The Wedding Chapel at the Celestial Palace Hotel.

That was interesting. She hadn't realized that the hotel had a chapel. *Only in Vegas.*

"It's so sweet of you to offer," Sofia said. "But it's your wedding night. Couldn't you drink it on your way to the airport?"

The bride put her hand over her mouth and shook her head. "That wouldn't be a good idea. We have been drinking champagne all day. I wanted to give it to someone who would enjoy it. So here, please take it."

The bride placed the bottle in Sofia's hands.

"Come on," said the groom, who was already edging away. "We need to go, or we're going to miss our flight."

"Thanks," Harris told them. "Good luck, you two. Many wishes for a happy life."

There was something sobering about the weight of the bottle in Sofia's hands and Harris's wishes for the happy couple. She hated herself for the way she was inwardly scoffing.

"Yeah, you might be happy now, but just wait. Marriage is hard. It's just not meant to last."

Harris leaned in. "What did you say?"

Damn. Had she said that out loud? She hadn't meant to.

"This has been so much fun, Harris, but I need some air. In fact, I think I'm ready to call it a night."

"I'll call the car to take us back to the hotel," Harris said after they had exited the nightclub. "It will only take a moment."

"I appreciate the offer, but I could really use a walk." The carefree woman who had been dancing with her arms over her head was gone, replaced by someone who looked like she'd been handed a piece of bad news. "This is the first time since I arrived for the convention that I've gotten out of the hotel. I couldn't forgive myself if I didn't walk the Strip at night. If you'd rather ride, please go ahead. I can make it back to the hotel on my own. It's not too far."

She gestured toward the Celestial Palace's revolving doors with the champagne. Then she blinked at the bottle as if she'd just remembered she was holding it.

She held it out to Harris.

"Here, take this," she said. "I'm leaving tomorrow, and I won't drink it before then."

"Then let's drink it now." He smiled, but her expression remained impassive and her gaze dropped back to the bubbly.

"We don't have any glasses," she reminded him, "and we can't exactly swig from the bottle. That would be real classy." Before he could offer a solution, she held out her hand like a traffic cop demanding a hard stop. "And please do not suggest that we take it back to your room because, while I've had a lovely time with you tonight, that's not going to happen. So, this seems like the perfect time to call it a night."

His brows shot up and his mouth fell open.

"You thought I was going to suggest that we take it back to my room?"

He did his best to feign surprise, even though he couldn't think of a better nightcap than he and Sofia enjoying the champagne—*and each other*—back in his suite.

She smirked. "Yeah, don't act so innocent. I know your type, Fortune."

"You do?" he challenged softly. "What exactly is my type, Sofia?"

To her credit, she wasn't exactly wrong. He'd love a night with her that involved champagne and exploring the tempting curves hidden under that dress. But the reality was, once they got back to Texas, the chances of them seeing each other were slim to none. Oh, they'd surely run into each other—Emerald Ridge was a small town—but his stay there was temporary.

He lived in Dallas, and she had kids, and she seemed to be as big a workaholic as he was. It just didn't seem like an intimate night like this would present itself again.

But they still had the walk back to the hotel.

"Fair enough," he said. "But I have an idea. Wait right here."

Her brow furrowed.

He took a couple of steps away and then turned back to her. "Don't leave, okay? I'll be right back."

Finally, a smile broke free and transformed her beautiful face. "What are you up to now?"

The cloud that had descended over her after the couple had offered them the champagne seemed to be lifting. He wasn't going to let the moment get away from them.

He returned a minute later, holding two large red Solo cups.

"I tried to buy two champagne glasses for us, but apparently there's a law against glass containers on the Strip and they didn't have plastic flutes. There's not an open container law. We can take a to-go cup, but we'll have to settle for these. The concierge must get asked for cups a lot because she had them below the desk." He grinned. "The good news is they're so large that they can hold the entire bottle split between the two of them."

She laughed. "I can't drink that much champagne. Not after all that wine we had with dinner and the cocktail we had in the club."

He popped the cork and started filling the first cup. "Just enjoy what you want."

Looking resigned, Sofia took the cup, shrugged and held it up in cheers to him.

"To a beautiful and most unexpected night," he said.

Sofia watched him over the rim of her cup as she took a sip.

"Shall we go?" Harris offered his arm. She accepted it.

"You are a persuasive man, Harris Fortune."

Outside, the Strip surrounded them in a dazzling display of lights and colors, a river of neon and people winding through the heart of the desert. He breathed in the scent of the city—a blend of exhaust, perfume and a hint of something sweet— filled his nostrils. He was tempted to lean in and see if that delectable scent was Sofia's shampoo. Instead, he took a long pull from his red cup.

The hum of traffic and the honking horns melded with the revelry of tourists and iconic city sounds, creating a symphony of Las Vegas Strip nightlife.

The Strip was pulsing with life. Street performers drew small crowds, their acts ranging from impressive to bizarre. A man in a sparkling Elvis costume posed for photos, while further down, a magician made cards disappear and reappear to the delight of onlookers.

Despite the constant motion of people, Harris felt a strange sense of calm wash over him. As he walked with Sofia, the Strip's chaos faded into the background. He couldn't remember the last time he was this relaxed. As he put a hand on the small of her back to guide her around a group of people who had stopped to take a selfie, she glanced up at him. Her cheeks were flushed and her eyes sparkled.

"Okay, I'm sorry, I have to know. How did you arrange for that song to come on when we walked into Gem?"

He squinted at her. "What song?"

"What song?" She made an impatient clicking noise with her tongue. "The Cher song that we were talking about at dinner. We walked into Gem and it started playing. Like magic."

She stopped, somehow getting in front of him and giving him an amazed, mouth-open, palms-up shrug. "How?"

It was just dumb luck, but if she thought he'd arranged it, what could it hurt to play along?

He quirked a brow. "Would I get extra points if I did make it happen?"

"Possibly."

"And what would those extra points get me?" he asked.

He fully expected her to backhand him in the chest or make some kind of declaration that drew the line. Instead, she took a long pull on her red cup and then pursed her lips. "Let me get back to you on that."

"I'll be right here." He took her hand and they started walking again. She didn't pull away and the feel of her hand in his did something weird to his insides. It made him feel all warm and off-kilter, but he liked it.

She made him feel all warm and off-kilter. That's why he didn't want this night to end.

"Do you come to the hair show every year? Are you a regular?"

"Hardly." As they passed the Bellagio and its famous dancing fountains, a breeze blew across the water. She reached up and brushed a strand of dark hair out of her eyes. "After I opened The Style Lounge, I used to come to the convention pretty regularly, but I haven't been in a while. Dan used to resent it when I'd come. It got to be one of those things that was easier to eliminate than fight about. This year, after the divorce, I decided to treat myself. It was sort of symbolic, you know. But you don't want to hear about that—"

Sofia stopped suddenly and turned toward the street. Her hand pulled out of his. It sort of felt like he'd lost a part of himself.

"There it is." She pointed across the busy street to the Eiffel Tower replica at Paris Las Vegas. Its blue, white and red lights twinkling to rival the Bellagio fountains behind them.

"That's what I really wanted to see," she said. "I mean, I know the real one is in Paris, but if I squint my eyes, I can pretend like I'm there. Even if it's just for a minute."

She sighed and leaned into him, fitting perfectly in the crook where his arm and body met. He put his arm around her.

"Have you ever been to Paris?" Harris asked.

Without taking her gaze off the tower, she shook her head wistfully. "I'll get there someday. I have a passport, but, realistically, I probably won't go until after my kids are grown."

"If we leave right now, we could be there in about eleven hours." He took a sip and watched her over the rim of his cup.

She looked up at him and rolled her eyes. "Right."

She matched his sip.

"You don't believe me," he murmured.

She shook her head.

"All I have to do is call my pilot and he'll file the flight plan and have the plane ready by the time we check out of the hotel and get to the airport."

"You own a plane." It was a statement, not a question.

"Sure. I travel a lot."

"I'll bet most women think that's pretty sexy," she said.

He winked. "All that matters is whether *you* think I'm sexy."

Her eyes flashed in a way that didn't exactly say no, and he was pretty good at reading people, but she didn't answer him. Instead, she leaned into him more and took another long sip as they stood there together, gazing at the iconic monument.

"This champagne is a lot better than I thought it would be." Her words were slow and rounded at the edges, and an accent he didn't realize she had was beginning to break through her polished style of speaking. It made him want to stay like this forever.

When was the last time he'd thought that way about a woman?

It had been ages, that's for sure. But that's how he was feeling right now, with her standing so close, pressing into him.

The realization had his mind spinning.

"I'll bet you can talk most women into just about anything once they learn you have a private plane, huh?"

He blinked. "What?"

"You heard me."

"What makes you think I'd be interested in a woman who was only interested in me for my plane?"

"Well, you're the one who was dangling it out there for me to see—"

She snapped her lips shut and clapped her hand over her mouth, but not before a giggle slipped out. "Never mind. That didn't come out right. It sounded a little bit dirty, didn't it."

Harris laughed, too. "Good because I'm pretty discriminating about who I dangle for."

She laughed. "*Shhhhhhh!* Stop."

She turned to face him. Standing on her tiptoes, she leaned in and pressed her finger to his lips. *"Shhhhhhh,"* she said again. "That just sounded wrong."

His arms slid around her as naturally as if they'd finally found their home.

She was laughing so hard that some of the liquid from her glass sloshed over the side.

"Look what you made me do," she chided through the laughter. "This is too good to waste."

"You're right." Before he could stop himself, he took her hand, raised it to his lips and lapped the liquid off the inside of her wrist. Then he turned her hand over and kissed the top of it.

The next thing he knew, their lips had found each other.

Their mouths fit together as perfectly as she'd fit under his arm…and he instinctively knew that their bodies would synchronize just as well together when they finally made love.

It was the kind of perfection that he wanted in his bed every night.

In his *life* every day.

The faint sound of a catcall whistle and someone hooting, "Get a room!" brought him back down to earth.

Maybe the champagne was affecting him more than he realized because he had no idea how long they'd been standing there like that on the Strip, tasting and exploring each other. All he knew was as they broke the kiss, Sofia's arms stayed around his neck and he liked it.

"That was nice," she murmured. "If I didn't have to get back to my kids tomorrow, I'd call your bluff and say, *Okay, Fortune, fire up that plane and sweep me away to Paris*."

Resting his forehead against hers, he said, "How about a City of Love rain check, then?"

"City of Love? *Bleeek*. Nope. Just Paris. There's no such thing as love. Don't ruin Paris for me by linking it with love."

"I'm not the one who came up with the name *City of Love*, but it's a bona fide thing."

"Yeah, but isn't it also called the City of Light?" she countered and took a step backward, away from him, a little unsteady on her feet. He grabbed her hand. She probably wouldn't have fallen if he hadn't steadied her, but he wanted to maintain that connection.

Suddenly, she pulled away. "You know what? If I did believe in love— But I don't. It's still a hard no for Sofia. 'Cause I've been through it, and it's like the worst kind of bait and switch, you know. It's a real gut punch. Been there done that and I'm never gonna do it again."

"Wait, but what were you going to say?" he asked.

She blinked at him and shook her head. "I said it. I don't believe in love."

"No, you said, and I quote—" He made air quotes with his fingers. "You said, *You know what? If I did believe in love—*"

He made a circular go-on gesture with his hands. "If you did believe in love... What? You can't just dangle something like that out there and not finish it."

She gave him a meaningful look. Her eyes were bloodshot, but she looked more beautiful right now than she had all night.

He was...smitten. The thought made him laugh out loud.

She smiled. "What are you laughing at?"

When he didn't answer, she planted a featherlight kiss on his lips.

"I have ways of making you talk, Fortune."

"I'll bet you do. But I have another idea. Will you trust me?"

"That depends. Does it involve flying to Paris tonight?"

"That's a good one, but no," he said. "Not tonight. But what if we made a wager? We're in Vegas. I haven't gambled yet. Have you?"

"I'm not a gambler," she informed him. "It's a waste of time and money. Just like love."

"Which brings me back to my point. To my wager. I'll bet I can prove that love really does exist. If I can't prove it, I'll pay for you to go to Paris anytime you want. If I can...well, that's self-explanatory. You either leave Vegas with a new outlook on love or a trip to Paris. Either way, you win. Are you in?"

The lights from the Eiffel Tower shone in her beautiful brown eyes. "But what's in it for you?" she asked.

Harris took her hand. "Come on. I'll show you."

Chapter Three

Sofia's head was pounding like a subwoofer in a teenager's car.

It took every ounce of effort she possessed to crack open one eye and glance at the clock on the nightstand: 6:37 a.m.

She pressed both palms to her eyes as she tried to remember last night, but she couldn't think past the sensation that someone was stabbing an icepick through her temple.

As she pulled her hands down her face, something scraped her left cheekbone.

She forced her eyes open, squinting through the sliver of the morning sun streaming in through the space where the curtains didn't meet, only to discover a gold ring on her finger.

Her left hand.

What in the world?

She'd taken her wedding ring off before she'd come to Las Vegas.

For that matter, this wasn't her wedding ring. The one Dan had given her had been a thin gold band. This one was at least a half-inch wide.

She tried to remove it, but her fingers were swollen. Probably a byproduct of all that alcohol. It had been a long time since she'd overindulged like that.

Pressing her palms to her eyes, she tried to recall the events of last night.

She'd gone to dinner with Harris Fortune. They'd had a lot of wine.

Then they went dancing.

That was fun.

But she shouldn't have had that cocktail—some kind of a rum punch that had tasted so good and had gone down way too easily.

This morning, the memory of it made her stomach churn like a reprimand.

And there was the champagne that the bride and groom had given them.

She knew she shouldn't have drunk it. But she had.

The details of last night were slowly unfolding. How they'd taken that champagne and— She gasped.

Had they really been kissing in front of the Eiffel Tower?

What if one of the product reps had seen her?

Oooh... She squeezed her eyes shut.

At least it hadn't been in Emerald Ridge.

As if. She never went out at home. Not for a night like that.

A night with Harris Fortune.

But wait...

A vague memory prodded the recesses of her mind. Something about Harris promising to prove to her that love was real.

Maybe it was a dream?

After all, they had been ridiculously tipsy...

No. They'd been flat-out *drunk*.

She rubbed her temples, trying to quell the pounding headache.

That seemed to unleash another memory of them at the Happy Days Insta Wedding Chapel.

She remembered Harris telling her he'd marry her right then and there to prove to her that love and a good marriage were about the right person.

Had they actually gotten married? *No.* Ay dios mío. *Please, no.*

Something shifted beside her, and for the first time since she'd opened her eyes, she looked over and saw Harris asleep beside her.

Oh no, this wasn't happening.

No. They didn't. She couldn't—

But, oh yes, they had.

The two of them had gone back to her hotel room and made mad, passionate love, which would explain why she was naked.

Please, please, please let us have used protection.

Sofia sat up, peering around to see if there was any evidence of it on the nightstand.

She didn't find that, but what she did see was an official-looking piece of paper.

With a shaking hand and a sinking feeling, she picked it up.

This is to certify that Sofia Gomez Simon and Harris Richmond Fortune were united in marriage on this day, October 4, in the year of 2025. Witnessed by Susan Campbell and Frank Allen.

Both Sofia and Harris had signed the certificate.

The fuzzy, foggy memory of them doing so came flooding back.

The scream started deep in her chest and clawed its way up. Sofia clamped her free hand over her mouth to stifle it, but to no avail.

She jumped out of bed, pulling the sheet with her.

"What? What's going on? What's wrong?"

Harris jolted upright and sat there looking around the hotel room, frowning and blinking like he was trying to get his bearings. He looked as disoriented as she felt.

"How could you?" she growled.

He pressed both hands to his head, but then it was as if he realized he was sitting there naked. He grabbed one of the bed pillows—her pillow—and covered himself.

"Do you mind?" he growled back.

"Yes, I *do* mind," she said.

"You asked me to stay."

She waved the marriage certificate at him.

"Wha...what is that?"

"It appears to be a marriage certificate, Harris. What did you do?"

"What did *I* do?" He blinked and, brow furrowed, held his hand out to her, motioning with his fingers for her to hand over the piece of paper.

Pulling the sheet higher, she leaned forward and handed it to him.

He studied it for a moment and then nodded.

"It seems we got married last night," he said matter-of-factly.

"What do you mean it *seems* that we got married? Either we did, or we didn't, and if you don't remember, then we'd better find out for sure and get this taken care of this morning because I have a plane to catch this afternoon. And I can't go home married to you."

He raised his brows, and somehow, he seemed a little wounded by her words. He was probably just hungover, but still, she didn't need to be mean.

"It's not just you, Harris. I can't be married to anyone. I just divorced my children's father. I can't go off to Vegas and come home with a new husband. What kind of a mother do you think I am?"

He opened his mouth as if he was going to say something but stopped. He closed his eyes, trying to gather his thoughts, before saying, "Look, I'm pretty hung over. This headache is not helping me think straight. Let me go back to my room, shower and take some aspirin."

Was he *serious*? There weren't enough painkillers in the world to make this situation go away.

Harris glanced at the clock on the nightstand next to him. "Why don't we meet for breakfast in Pauley's restaurant downstairs at eight? We can discuss the situation with clearer heads."

"There's nothing to discuss—unless it's how we're going to get to the annulment office. So we might as well get this fixed and pretend like it never happened. I thought the clerk wasn't supposed to issue marriage licenses to drunk people."

He quirked a brow at her. "Clearly, they didn't believe we were inebriated."

The vague memory of a pretty blonde who had been flirting with Harris last night popped into Sofia's head. She'd stood behind the counter in an office of some sort. It had to have been where they'd gotten their license.

Why was a woman in a marriage license office flirting with a man who was getting hitched? Clearly, the woman had been too busy making eyes at Harris to realize that they were in no state to take this step.

Making eyes?

Now she was channeling Abuela Rosa.

She sniffed and wrapped the sheet around her like a toga. "Let's just go get this over with. I have a plane to catch."

"You do know it's Sunday, right? Even if the marriage license bureaus are open seven days a week, it doesn't mean other municipal offices are."

"And you know this for a fact?" she challenged.

"No, I don't know this for a fact. Why would I know this? I've never gotten married before. Look, I have a headache. I need a shower and some time to think."

He tossed the pillow aside and stood up in all his glory.

She hated herself for it, but her gaze dropped and meandered the long, lean expanse of his perfect body—those perfect broad shoulders she'd leaned on last night, those perfectly muscled biceps that had held her so tight, that perfect six-pack, all the way down to...to the perfection that had rocked her world last... Several times.

Her face flamed and her mouth went even drier.

As she remembered how they'd moved together in a rhythm that made the rest of the world fall away, she thought about how the lovemaking had been at once tender and passionate. They'd fit together like they were made for each other. It had only been the two of them... And the promise Harris had made that he would prove to her that love really did exist.

But sex was *not* love.

Even as perfect as sex with Harris Fortune had been.

"You're staring." He picked up his trousers and disappeared into the bathroom, leaving her with a million questions swimming around in her head. At the top of the list was what he had meant when he'd said he could prove that love really did exist.

And how in the world had that led to them getting married?

Why couldn't she remember?

She wasn't much of a drinker, and last night she'd overdone it, but never in her life had she blacked out...and ended up married to a man she barely even knew.

A queasy uneasiness made the room spin and tilt out from under her. What was left of her equilibrium went with it.

She sat down on the edge of the bed and forced herself to draw in great gulps of air, letting them out in slow, measured gusts. Until finally, Harris—*her husband*—came back into the room fully dressed and looking way too good, in comparison to how crappy she felt—

About everything.

"You okay?" he asked. "Can I get you anything?"

"Harris, all I remember is drinking way too much and you telling me that you could prove that love really did exist. And the next thing I know, I'm waking up with a gold band on my finger and a souvenir marriage certificate from the Happy Days Insta Wedding Chapel."

He nodded. She noticed that he was wearing a gold band that matched hers.

Even though she wanted to take hers off and throw it at him or out the window—anywhere that she didn't have to see it—she couldn't bring herself to do it yet. Besides, if she lifted her arms, her makeshift toga might unravel.

That was the last thing she needed right now.

"All I want is for you to fill in the blanks for me," she said. "Can you at least do that? Please?"

"Yes. Of course. Now that I've had a chance to wake up, I do remember what happened last night. You seemed to be all for it, Sofia. You even called the marriage our *Great Experiment*."

She scowled at him.

"I did not. You lured me to the chapel to show me the happy people who were getting married."

"Right. After the first couple said I do and the chapel started playing, *I Can't Help Falling In Love With You*, you beelined to the lobby and started looking at rings."

"I did not."

"Yes, you did. I wanted to get you a diamond, but you kept insisting that you didn't want diamonds. You just wanted true love. You said, 'Let's give it a try, Fortune. Let's get married. It'll be our *Great Experiment*.'"

Suddenly, it all came flooding back to her.

Her hand flew to her mouth.

"I remember. Oh, Harris... Why didn't you say no and talk some sense into me?"

His look was impassive. "So, it's my fault now?"

She had the good grace to look away.

At least he'd tried to sleep on the couch, saying he wanted both of them to be sober the first time they made love, but she'd climbed on top of him and... Well, basically, she'd ridden him like the bull at Gilley's.

He was a good guy, an honorable man, but she couldn't be married.

She just *couldn't*.

It wasn't fair to either of them.

He got her a bottle of water, some crackers and a packet of painkillers from the minibar.

"Here, eat these and drink this to rehydrate. Get something in your stomach before you take the aspirin. Then why don't you take a shower and get dressed, and meet me in the restaurant downstairs? We'll figure things out."

An hour later, Harris was sitting in a booth in Pauley's restaurant, freshly showered and shaved, and feeling more like himself. Or as much like himself as he could feel after waking up in Vegas married.

What had gotten into him last night?

It didn't matter now. Rather than beating himself up, he needed to focus on making things right.

Sofia had indicated she was on board with an annulment. That was good. Neither of them wanted to be married right now.

She had just gotten out of one marriage.

He certainly didn't want his first marriage to end in divorce so soon after getting married. He wanted to fall in love and spend the rest of his life with the love of his life.

Right now, an annulment was the only way to go. To that end, when he'd gotten back to his room, he'd called his lawyer for advice. Unfortunately, the man had said that it wasn't as easy to annul a Vegas wedding as it was to get hitched there. He'd added since family law wasn't his specialty, Harris should consult an attorney who specialized in that practice. He promised Harris he'd give him a referral tomorrow since most law offices weren't open on the weekend.

Family law.

The words ping-ponged around Harris's brain as he sipped his coffee and waited for Sofia.

Family. Was that what they were now? *A family?*

How could they be a family when they barely knew each other?

When he'd sat down at the restaurant, he'd ordered two coffees before it had dawned on him that he didn't even know if Sofia drank coffee.

Even though she'd been interesting and there was no doubt that he was attracted to her, he didn't know her.

In fact, for all he knew, she could be another Amanda, who was simply after the Fortune name and money.

He'd dodged a bullet when that relationship had ended. If he'd learned nothing else from it, he thought it would've made him more careful.

In hindsight, he saw the red flags that should've been obvious last night: Sofia had protested too much. She'd been steadfast about not believing in love and marriage, yet by the end of the night, she'd married him.

However, in all fairness, she was the one who'd first brought up the annulment. His gut was telling him Sofia was no Amanda. Only time would tell.

As he poured the last of the coffee from the carafe into his cup, he glanced at his watch and realized he'd been waiting for nearly an hour. A queue was starting to form at the hostess stand.

He took out his cell phone and called the hotel's front desk.

"Sofia Gomez Simon's room, please."

A moment later, the operator said, "I'm sorry, sir, but she has checked out."

Checked out and then coming to breakfast? Or checked out, leaving him high and dry?

He had a feeling he knew the answer.

Doing his best to tamp down the irritation roiling in his gut, he pulled out his wallet and left some bills on the table—enough to cover the cost of the coffee and a generous tip since he'd occupied the table for so long.

Now what? he pondered as he stood in the lobby looking around, giving Sofia one last benefit of the doubt that she wouldn't just ditch him like this. But he knew she was probably already on her way to the airport.

"What do you mean you don't have any cars?" Sofia said to the harried-looking attendant behind the rental car desk. "Cars are your business. How can you not have any? I have waited in line for more than an hour."

"I'm sorry, ma'am, a bunch of flights were canceled this morning. We've had more business than we anticipated."

"I know about the canceled flights," she huffed. "Mine

was one of them. That's why I'm here. I have to get home. Isn't there anything you can do?"

The woman shot her a sympathetic look that Sofia figured masked the urge to say, *You and everyone else.* "I'm happy to add you to the waiting list. I can call you if we have cancellations."

Before Sofia could answer the woman, her cell phone rang. She didn't recognize the number, but in hopes that it might be the airline calling with the good news that they'd found a flight that took off before 11:00 p.m., she answered it.

"This is Sofia Gomez Simon."

"It sure is," said a familiar voice that made her already sensitive stomach lurch.

"Did you forget that we were meeting for breakfast this morning?" he asked.

"Hello, Harris. I'm sorry. I should've let you know that I decided to leave for the airport early. I sincerely apologize."

"Ma'am, I'm sorry to interrupt," said the rental car agent. "But could you please step aside so I can assist the next person in line?"

Sofia held up a finger. "I'm so sorry. Please just give me one minute because I would like to add my name to the waiting list. Or maybe you could check and see if another one of your offices has a car. I can take an Uber to get there."

"Where are you Ubering to?" Harris asked.

"Look, I can't talk right now. My flight was canceled—and apparently, everyone else's was, too. The next flight is late tonight. I'm trying to rent a car so I can get home to my kids."

"You do realize it's a seventeen-hour drive from Las Vegas to Emerald Ridge, right?"

Sofia blinked. She hadn't had time to look up the distance. She'd just joined the stampede from the gate to the rental car office. Well, clearly, driving wouldn't work. If she took the 11:00 p.m. flight, she'd still get home sooner than if she drove.

She stepped aside and murmured her apologies to the family behind her before turning to the agent. "Looks like I won't be needing a car after all. Thanks for your help."

"Okay, Harris. I need to go. I'm going to see if I can get on that 11:00 p.m. flight. I'll talk to you tomorrow about what we need to do to rectify this situ—"

As she turned with her suitcase, she ran into the very solid chest of Harris Fortune.

"What the—" Her cheeks flamed. "Harris, what are you doing here?"

She disconnected the call and stuffed her phone into her handbag, using it as an excuse to regain her composure. All she could think was that she was married to this man.

But not really. It didn't count if she didn't remember it, right?

Ah, but the problem was she *did* remember it. As the day had worn on and the fog from her hangover had lifted, bits and pieces of last night and their *Great Experiment* were coming into focus.

"I came to find you," Harris said. "We left it that you were supposed to meet me at Pauley's for breakfast. If you wanted to eat at the airport, you should've told me rather than ghosting me."

"I didn't ghost you. I… I needed some time to think. You were right. All the agencies that could undo this mess we've gotten ourselves into are closed on Sundays. Though that hardly seems fair since they leave the trap door to getting married wide open seven days a week so that anyone can unwittingly fall into it." She knew she needed to stop talking, but she couldn't seem to find a period. Harris was just standing there listening to her spew. He was nodding like he was taking it all in. "Anyhow, all of that is beside the point. I need to get home to my kids. Now that I know it's a seventeen-hour drive, I need to get on that eleven o'clock flight and then call my husband and—"

"*I'm* your husband," he reminded her. "Dan is your ex-husband. Or at least I assume you were talking about Dan since I'm standing right in front of you and there's no need for you to call me."

"Yes, he's my ex-husband. I need to call Dan and let him know that my flight has been canceled." She started walking, hoping that Harris would just leave her alone, but of course, he followed. When he caught up with her, she said, "And for the record, you are *not* my husband."

"*Au contraire, mon cheri.* We're legally married and that not only makes me your husband, but it also means you're my wife. And one of the perks of being my wife is that you have access to a private plane, which could have you home in just under three hours once we're airborne."

She stopped walking. So did he.

"What are you talking about, Fortune?" she demanded.

He squinted at her. "Don't tell me you don't remember talking about my plane last night."

"Of course I do. I said you could probably talk a woman into anything once you got her on board your private plane."

"No, you said, *I'll bet you can talk most women into just about anything once they learn you have a private plane.* I don't invite many women onto my plane."

She quirked her brow at him. "Right, you said, and I quote, *What makes you think I'd be interested in a woman who was only interested in me for my plane?* I'm not interested in your plane, Harris. So, if you'll excuse me, I need to go get on that flight."

He followed her to the ticketing desk. She ignored him. Maybe if she pretended like he wasn't there, he'd go away.

By the time she'd waited in line and all was said and done, the eleven o'clock flight was full. The next available flight left seven hours later, at six o'clock in the morning.

They waited as the agent looked one more time for a better flight.

"Sofia, this is ridiculous. I'm leaving as soon as I know you've gotten your flight sorted, but my invitation still stands. I'm going to Dallas. There's no reason you can't fly with me. Unless you're stubborn and you'd rather wait for that 6:00 a.m. flight." He shrugged. "Your choice."

She exhaled a weary sigh. With each click of the keyboard, the woman behind the counter shook her head. It wasn't looking promising.

As he waited silently, Harris rubbed his chin with his left hand, and Sofia noticed the gold band on his ring finger. *Dammit!* He was still wearing that wedding ring. She'd yanked hers off and had stuck it in her purse before she'd left the hotel.

Would he still be so glib about this sham of a marriage once he fully realized she and the kids were a package deal?

"I'm sorry, Ms. Gomez Simon, the 6:00 a.m. flight is the best that I can do," said the agent. "Storms in other parts of the country have grounded planes and there were mechanical issues with others. It's caused quite a backlog. I'm happy to put you on this flight."

"I really need to get home to my children today," she insisted to Harris. "Dan said he has to be back in Austin by 6:00 p.m., which wouldn't have been a problem if my flight had been on time."

The fleeting thought of whether her ex was meeting the woman in the photo that Jacinta had texted her flitted through her mind, and she was tempted to make Dan wait, but she didn't know that for sure. And her ex was free to date. Just like she was free to marry the first man who wasn't Dan who'd taken her out to dinner.

"Look, I'm offering you a solution," Harris said. "What's it going to be?"

During the first hour of the flight back to Dallas, Sofia must've listed at least fifty reasons why love and marriage were for fools.

Harris let her talk and tried his best to keep his face neutral.

"And I'm no fool," she finally concluded.

"I didn't say you were," Harris said as he refilled her glass with sparkling water from the blue glass bottle sitting on the table between them. "Yet, here we are legally married. Man and wife. Maybe you have a subconscious need to be married. Did you ever consider that?"

She sat ramrod-straight in her seat. Her mouth fell open and she scrunched up her pert little nose as if she smelled something vile.

"Are you saying I purposely misled you? That *I* tricked you into getting married?" She shook her head and looked up at the ceiling, gesturing emphatically with her hands. "*I'll bet I can show you that love really does exist*, is what you said. You're the one who—" Rather than finish the sentence, she made a growling noise in her throat and sat back with a hard *umph*.

He laughed. He couldn't help it.

Was this woman this passionate about everything?

"And you think it's funny?" She pointed a finger at him. "You know, I'll bet you were the type of kid who, when your parents told you no, you badgered them until they gave in. You *were* that kid, weren't you?"

It was strange how her words landed like an unexpected punch to the gut. His parents had been gone for twenty years now. While the grief over losing them in that horrific plane crash wasn't fresh, every once in a while, in the most unexpected situations, it did sneak up and pull the rug out from under him.

Like now.

He'd finally gotten married—even if it wasn't in the most conventional way—and it probably wouldn't last. But his parents would never know his wife. And his kids—because he *did* want children someday—but they would never know their grandparents.

Still, he knew that the only way he would ever get back that sense of family he'd experienced before his parents had died was if he got married and had a family of his own. The realization washed over him that maybe he was more open to settling down and starting a family than he'd thought.

The problem was that finding the right person—a soulmate for life—had proven more difficult than he'd imagined.

He gazed at Sofia, who was staring at him intently, looking smug, as if her *badgering kid* label had put him in his place.

"My parents died when I was twelve," he said gruffly. "Death does funny things to your memory. I don't really remember if I was *that kid*, as you put it."

She bit her bottom lip and her eyes went huge.

"Harris, I'm so sorry. I had no idea. Otherwise, I wouldn't have said that."

Her inadvertent jab seemed to soften her because the rest of the way home, she made a real effort to be polite and talk about neutral subjects.

While it was nice to see a softer side of her, he had to admit he kind of had a thing for that spirited personality.

When he pulled up in front of her home, a neat arts-and-crafts bungalow with a manicured lawn and an orange-and-black Halloween wreath hanging on the wooden front door, he had a moment when he wished she would invite him in so that he could see what lay on the other side of that barrier.

"Harris, thank you," she said. "You really did save my life. I'm actually home early."

"Let me help you with your bag."

She protested, but he was out of the car, lifting it out of the trunk before she could stop him. He extended the retractable handle, ready to carry it up to the porch, when the front door flew open.

"Mommy!" cried a dark-haired little boy who looked young. Probably elementary school age, though Harris wasn't good at guessing kids' ages.

Sofia met him halfway, dropped down on one knee and enfolded the little kid in a hug.

"Is it already three o'clock?" he asked.

"No, sweetie, I caught an earlier flight because I missed you so much."

"I missed you, too," he said and hugged Sofia again. "I'm glad you're home."

Harris leaned on the suitcase handle and watched the scene unfold. It was touching to see how tender Sofia was with her child. Clearly, they shared a special bond.

A melancholy wistfulness pulled at his heart.

There was nothing like family.

While the boy was still in his mother's embrace, he looked up and his gaze locked with Harris's.

The boy pulled away and pointed. "Who's that?"

At a loss for how to explain, Sofia hugged the boy tighter.

* * *

Harris kept reminding himself that he didn't know much about Sofia except that she was divorced and owned a salon. She was fiercely protective of her children and talked about them with such pride. She was exactly the type of mother he wanted for his future children.

Wow. The irony of waking up married to a woman who seemed to tick so many of the boxes he wanted in a life partner, yet they both couldn't get away from this marriage fast enough. If he didn't know better, he might think that fate had brought them together.

He wheeled her suitcase up the walk and stopped next to Sofia. She stood and cast him a wary look. He tried to telegraph, *Don't worry, I'm not going to spill the beans.*

"Jackson Carlos, please go inside, and I'll be right along."

The boy took off running up the walk, bounding onto the porch, yelling, "Mommy's home! Mommy's home!"

"Thank you, Harris, for getting me home. I'd still be stuck in Vegas if you hadn't helped me out."

"At your service." He bowed his head respectfully.

Sofia cast a nervous glance at the front door. "I need to get inside, but the salon is closed tomorrow, and the kids will be in school. I'll be in touch in the morning so we can figure out how to undo this mess we're in. I…have your phone number since you called me."

She offered him a half smile, took her suitcase and turned toward the house.

As Harris climbed into his Porsche and started the engine, he heard a little girl's jubilant shouts of, *Mommy! You're home.* He cast one last glance before he pulled away and saw a man standing on the porch, looking at his car.

So that was the man who'd let Sofia get away.

Well, his loss just might be Harris's gain. Because he had a feeling he wasn't quite done here.

The most confirmed bachelor in Texas suddenly had a deep urge to prove something to Sofia about love and marriage; that it could work when you found the right person.

How would they know if they were right for each other if they didn't give it a try?

Clearly, she wasn't the same twenty-two-year-old who'd married her first boyfriend.

But Harris still held the same deeply rooted belief that marriage was sacred. His parents had made it work through good times and bad, and after they'd died, he'd vowed that he would, too. It was his way to honor them. After the near disaster with Amanda, the woman he almost married, he'd vowed to be careful. Careful had turned into reticence toward marriage—toward trusting himself.

As a businessman, once he settled on a course of action, he didn't abandon it because he thought it might be a mistake. He stood by his actions and gave it time to work before he changed course.

Maybe he needed to apply that principle here, and give this marriage a chance.

Chapter Four

"Was that Harris Fortune?" Dan asked as he stood on the porch watching the midnight-blue Porsche drive away.

Sofia's stomach lurched and she broke out into a cold sweat.

Dan knows Harris?

"Yes, it was. I didn't realize you knew him."

"I don't know him personally," he said as he commandeered her suitcase and wheeled it inside. "I worked for his cousin, Micah Fortune, for as long as we were married. Remember? How do you know him?"

Sofia tutted at Dan's sarcasm. "Why are you so interested?"

"Why are you being so defensive? Are you and Harris getting cozy?"

"I bumped into him at the airport, and he was nice to offer me a ride home."

Technically, that was the truth. She didn't owe Dan any more than that. Good grief, if he acted like that over her sharing a ride with the man, she didn't even want to think about what he'd do if he knew that she'd flown in on his private jet.

Or that they were *married*.

Her peripheral vision went a little white and fuzzy at the reminder.

This was too awkward.

NANCY ROBARDS THOMPSON61

Dan was her ex-husband. He had no right grilling her like that.

She wasn't breaking sacred vows by flying back with Harris...or sleeping with him.

Or marrying him.

It took every ounce of self-control she had not to tell Dan to mind his own business.

First and foremost, she didn't want to argue in front of the kids, but she also realized that snipping back at him over Harris would only make her look guilty.

"Riding with Harris saved money. Ubers are expensive," she said segueing to a different subject.

Dan took the bait beautifully.

"Yes, they are," he answered. "That's why I suggested you drive to the airport and park in long-term parking."

"Long-term parking is expensive, too," she countered, even though it would've been a tax write-off. "At least my car was at home in the garage rather than sitting out in the elements."

"But long-term parking is not as expensive as an Uber." The smirk on Dan's face irritated her.

Once again, she exercised great restraint, stopping just short of saying that her decision not to take her car had ultimately paid off because, thanks to Harris, she hadn't used the rideshare, and the return trip hadn't cost her a dime. But that would've brought them right back to square one and reopened the Harris interrogation.

Dan still couldn't seem to grasp this dominance that he tried to assert over her was one of the things that had ruined their marriage.

He always had to be right.

"You know what, Dan? You're right." She forced a smile. "And you'd better get on the road if you want to make it back to Austin before six o'clock."

Just let him have the last word, she told herself. It was no skin off her nose. Plus, he'd be too busy basking in his self-righteousness to ask her more questions.

Just as her stomach started to roil with resentment, the kids bounded up to him and he picked them up, one under each arm, and swung them around.

"I'm the big spinning giant and I've found me some tasty morsels that I'll whip up into a froth the faster I spin."

The kids squealed in delight and the ire Sofia felt a moment ago began to melt away.

Everything else aside, Dan was a good father. He loved his kids. He was always there for them. Kaitlin and Jackson adored their daddy.

At least they had that.

After Dan left, Sofia played a board game with the kids. They had dinner. The kids took baths, brushed their teeth and then laid out their school clothes for the next morning.

It was lights out at eight o'clock.

As Sofia set to work packing Jackson and Kaitlin's school lunches, the situation with Harris came flooding back to her. She'd been so involved with her children that she'd nearly forgotten what had transpired with the man over the weekend. But now that the house was silent and she was alone with her thoughts, it all came flooding back to her in a rush.

"What a punch to the gut," she muttered as she cut carrots into sticks and slathered whole-wheat bread with organic peanut butter and all-fruit grape jelly.

After she'd finished the lunches and stashed them in the refrigerator so they'd be ready to load into lunch boxes first thing in the morning, she brewed herself a cup of herbal tea, picked up her phone and settled on the couch in the living room.

It took her a few minutes to figure out what she wanted

to say—several tries typing out a message and then erasing it—but finally, she decided that the best way to get through this was to hit it head-on.

She wrote:

Good morning, it's Sofia. I'd like to meet first thing tomorrow (Monday) morning. My children will be at school until four o'clock, and the salon is closed. Please let me know your availability.

She winced at the message's cool tone. It could've been a to a client or a vendor. But this wasn't a love note or even a text to a friend. She didn't know him well enough to call him a friend…even though the feel of his body had imprinted in her memory.

"Stop it!" she said aloud.

They needed to get this taken care of as soon as possible. The best thing to do was to get right to work on cleaning up this mess they'd made rather than putting it off.

As she sipped her tea, she saw the three dots dance to life.

Tell me what time and where. I'll be there.

If anyone saw them together in Emerald Ridge, it was bound to raise eyebrows. So, Sofia had suggested they meet at the Paris Café, in Canterbury, which was about halfway between Emerald Ridge and Dallas—far enough away from curious busybodies.

The mindset in her hometown was if a single man and woman were spotted together, it had to mean there was something romantic brewing. Because no one in Emerald Ridge believed men and women could be just friends. Maybe she was exaggerating, but Sofia didn't want to take any chances.

The last thing she needed was for people to get the wrong idea or start asking questions and find out their secret.

When she turned into the parking lot, Harris's Porsche was already there, parked facing the road right under the café's Eiffel Tower sign.

Her first thought was, *Extra points for being early.*

But extra points for what? Maybe now that he'd had a minute to think about it, he'd be even more eager than she was to wipe the slate clean.

"I hope you've come armed with solutions, Fortune," she murmured aloud.

She stepped out of her bronze-colored Toyota Sienna minivan, feeling every bit the mother of two that she was, and gave herself a mental check as she paused to lock the vehicle's doors with a click of her key fob.

A mother of two was exactly who she was, and she was damn proud of it. Even if a minivan wasn't the hottest car—her gaze tracked to Harris's Porsche—her van was new-*ish* and safe, reliable transportation for her children.

So what if it wasn't sexy? She worked hard to afford it.

These days, *sexy* wasn't on her agenda...because look where one night of *hot and sexy* had landed her—smack-dab in the middle of a bogus, yet legally binding, marriage.

Nope. Hot and sexy were not her friends.

That was one of the reasons she'd dressed down this morning, opting for blue jeans, a rust-colored argyle sweater, and low, square-heeled ankle boots. She wasn't dressing for Harris Fortune. She was dressing for her day off. A day when she had a to-do list that was a lot longer than she'd ever dream of accomplishing today—especially after being out of town for three days and then taking the time to drive to Canterbury to meet with Harris.

When she stepped inside the café, he waved at her from a

corner booth. She did her best to ignore the way her traitorous stomach flipped at the sight of him. But with each step toward him, she grew more nervous.

So, she chalked the nerves up to the desperation of the situation.

Just be cool.

To that end, she kept her expression neutral as she slid into the booth, across from this man.

Her husband.

No. Her mistake.

Their *mistake. It took two to pull off a drunken Vegas wedding.*

And that's all it was.

That was the touchstone she would come back to if she lost sight of why they were there.

"Good morning." A broad smile spread across his handsome face. He was dressed in a pressed, blue Oxford-cloth shirt. As she'd walked up, she could see he was wearing khaki pants. No doubt, his version of casual.

Damn him. Why did he have to look so good?

"Good morning," she said, noticing that he was still wearing his wedding ring. She was opening her mouth to remind him to take it off when he asked, "How did you find this place?"

Sofia tore her gaze away from his hand and gave the café a cursory glance. She took in the inexpensive artwork on the walls that depicted various Paris landmarks—the Arc de Triomphe, the Louvre's glass pyramid, the Champs-élysées, and, of course, the large black-and-white photograph of the Eiffel Tower.

Her mind raced back to Saturday night on the Strip when she'd swooned at the sight of the Eiffel Tower replica.

For a nanosecond, she shrank a little at the possibility that he might think she was content to settle for cheap imitations of Paris rather than aspiring to see the real deal. She hadn't even thought of that when she'd suggested the Paris Café to him. What had mattered was that it was far enough out of town that they wouldn't run into anyone they knew.

"I have a friend who lives in Dallas," she said. "We meet here because it's halfway, and this place has good coffee." She shrugged. "Why? Is it not up to your standards?"

She hadn't meant to sound so defensive, but judging by the look on Harris's face, that was exactly how she'd come across.

"This place is fine. I was just curious how it had landed on your radar."

Silence hung between them like a lead curtain, thick and heavy.

"Well, now you know," she said. "By the way, why are you still wearing that ring?"

She nodded toward his left hand. He lifted his hand and flexed his fingers.

"I guess it felt so natural that I forgot to take it off."

He smiled.

She couldn't tell if he was serious or trying to yank her chain. Probably the latter.

"Unless you have a good explanation about why you're wearing a wedding ring that does not involve me or what happened in Vegas, I suggest you take it off."

His gaze lingered on his hand long enough that Sofia braced herself for an objection, but finally, he slid it off and stashed it in his wallet.

"I hope you'll be just as agreeable about the annulment," Sofia said.

Before Harris could answer, the server approached their table.

"Hey, there. What can I get for you?"

She was tall, blond and pretty. Her name tag said Becky. On the occasions that Sofia and her friend, Francine, had met at the café for coffee, Sofia hadn't seen the waitress there. Clearly, Becky hadn't seen her, either, as she directed the words to Harris. In fact, she couldn't seem to take her eyes off him.

"I'd like a cup of black coffee, please," Sofia said.

The woman did a double take as if noticing Sofia for the first time. "You sure I can't get you anything else to go with that? We have some delicious apple pie. All of our baked goods are made fresh on the premises."

"Just coffee, thanks."

Becky nodded and her gaze—and smile—shifted back to Harris. "How 'bout you, hon?"

"Coffee, and I'll take a piece of that pie, please," he said. "You sold me on it, and you might as well bring two forks in case my wife changes her mind."

Becky's gaze fell to Harris's bare ring finger. "Aw, that's so sweet. How long have y'all been married?"

"We're newlyweds," Harris announced, reaching across the table and taking hold of Sofia's hand. "Still on our honeymoon…"

Sofia's face flamed. He was baiting her, and she wasn't going to give him the pleasure of letting him know he was rattling her.

"Aw, y'all make such a cute couple. I'll be right back with your pie. And those two forks."

When they were alone again, Sofia pulled her hand out of his, leaned forward and looked him in the eyes. "Look, Harris, can you just not… What if she knows someone we know?"

"You're the one who picked this place because it was out of the way."

"Okay, let's just get to the point. Please tell me that you

have some good news about the annulment. And look." She
put her hand on his arm. "This isn't personal, but as you know,
I just got divorced, and I can't be married again. Not to you.
Not to anyone. I just can't."

"I understand," he said, "but, unfortunately, it looks like
you're going to be stuck with me for a while."

Harris watched Sofia's face pale.

Then she drew in a deep breath and seemed to reset her
resolve.

"Come on, Harris," she said. "Stop with the jokes."

"I'm sorry, but I'm not joking. First thing this morning, I
called the firm that my attorney recommended, and the lawyer who would handle our case is out of town for ten days."

Sofia huffed. "Well, then find another lawyer. Dallas is a
big city. I'm sure he's not the only person around here who
practices family law."

"*She's* the best one to get you what you want."

"What *we* want," she corrected. "We're in this together,
and we'll get out of it together."

His thumb went to the bare place on his left ring finger
where the wedding band had been. He had to admit that he
kind of missed the feel of that ring on his finger. His hand
felt naked without it.

What was happening to him?

"I guess I'm not as freaked out as you seem to be," he said.

"And why aren't you, Harris? You should be *very* freaked
out." Her voice went up an octave. "You're married to a
woman you don't even know."

He shrugged. "I have a sense about people. It's a skill that's
helped me in life, and that same gut feeling is telling me that
you and I could work."

"What? *Why?*" she sputtered.

"You've got to admit that our wedding night was pretty damn good."

That was the truth.

She bit her bottom lip before saying, "You are depraved. You don't even know me. Is this a case of just wanting something you think you can't have? I'm saying I don't want to be married to you. So you know, you're all in because of the thrill of the chase."

Deciding to use some reverse psychology, he shrugged. "Hmm, I hadn't thought about that. Why don't you try me?"

She flinched. "I have no idea what you're talking about."

"Pretend like you're happy about this marriage. Pretend for a moment like you're in love with me, and you want this marriage even more than I do. Let me see if it makes me change my mind."

Their gazes connected for a moment and Harris felt a zing of attraction that made him believe that his gut really might be trying to tell him something.

It should've been telling him this was totally insane.

Sofia sat back in the booth, crossing her arms over the front of her and rolling her eyes. "Don't be ridiculous."

The server chose that moment to deliver the coffee and pie.

"I forgot to ask you if you'd like a slice of cheddar melted over the top of the pie," Becky said. "I know it sounds weird, but it's real good. I didn't believe it until Sally, the owner of this place—and she's also the chef who makes all these goodies—made me taste it and see for myself."

Becky put a hand on her hip. "It would just take me a minute. What do ya say?"

"Thanks, but I'm just a simple guy who likes his apple pie plain and his coffee black," Harris said.

Sofia snorted.

When both Harris and Becky looked at her, she flinched

a little bit as if she hadn't meant to make the sound out loud. So she picked up her coffee cup and took a long pull. But that hardly helped ease the awkwardness because she coughed and winced and set down the cup with a clatter.

Her hand flew to her lips. "That was hot."

"Careful there, hon," Becky said. "That coffee is from a fresh pot. It's steaming hot. I'm sorry. I shoulda warned ya."

Sofia held up her hand. "It's not your fault."

"You want some ice?" Becky offered.

"No, thank you," Sofia said. "I'll just let the coffee cool for a bit before I take another sip."

Becky glanced back and forth between the two of them as if intuiting that she'd interrupted something. "Well, okay then, I'll leave you two newlyweds alone. Just wave me down if ya need anything."

As soon as Becky was out of earshot, Sofia snorted again. "Just a simple guy who has his own driver in Vegas and a pilot to fly his private plane."

When he started to protest, she raised her hand.

"Let's stay on topic. Surely, you know other lawyers."

"No, Cathy Henderson is the best. I'll be honest with you, my lawyer warned me that the courts don't just dole out annulments. He said that we should prepare ourselves for the request not to be granted."

"Why?" Panic flashed in her big brown eyes. "Drunken vows are grounds for annulment! Or at least they should be. And why do you look so calm?"

"I'm just telling you what my lawyer said. That's why he's referred us to Cathy Henderson, but as I said, she's out of town right now."

"Fine. I'll find someone myself and get the process started. I probably should've done that rather than waiting for you to handle it."

"I'll level with you," he said. "If we can't get an annulment I'm not sure I want a divorce."

"What's wrong with a divorce?" she demanded.

"An annulment makes the situation go away," he said. "A divorce remains on the record."

"Oh, I see. You don't want your image tainted by divorce. Fortune, need I remind you that you're married to a woman who *is* divorced?"

"If you would've let me finish what I was saying, you would've heard that I don't want a divorce before we give our marriage a chance to work out. It doesn't matter to me that you're divorced—"

He stopped himself before saying that he was lucky she was divorced because if she'd been married, he would've never asked her to dinner in Vegas and they would've never had the chance to...

The thought—no, this *feeling* that he was smitten—made him realize yet again that he was not done here. No, not at all. He suddenly had a deep urge to prove something to Sofia about love and marriage—that it could work. He wanted to know her better, or at least, he didn't want to let her go before they'd given their marriage—as unconventional as it was—a fair shake.

Yes. That was what he wanted, and that realization nearly knocked the air out of him.

He thought he'd found that once in Amanda. He'd almost married her, but he'd learned that she hadn't been truthful about what she'd wanted out of their life together. After a couple of years of pretending to share all of his interests and values, once she'd had a ring on her finger and they were planning their life together, the truth had come out.

She'd wanted all the things his money could buy and all the advantages that came with the Fortune name, but she hadn't wanted to be a mother. Placating him, she'd said *if* they had children, she would prefer to use a surrogate because she didn't want to wreck her figure, and she would need at least one full-time nanny to deal with the little monsters.

Little monsters.

He couldn't get the sound of her voice saying those words out of his head. This person who had revealed herself just weeks before the wedding was not the woman she had pretended to be to make him fall in love.

On the other hand, the woman who was sitting in front of him—*his wife*—wasn't the least bit impressed with his money or a lifestyle that could be hers by virtue of marriage.

She was more concerned about her children and living an honest life.

In theory, *that* was the kind of woman he always thought he wanted to be married to.

After Amanda, after he'd been such a bad judge of character, he thought he'd never let anyone get this close. While he'd dated a lot of women since then—and many of them had tried to make him commit—the Amanda mistake had him guarding his heart with extra vigilance.

Now, he realized it was as if he'd been viewing life through a piece of bulletproof glass. He could see what he wanted so clearly on the other side, but he didn't know how to break through to get there.

Maybe he shouldn't give up so easily.

He realized she was squinting at him. "What are you getting at, Harris?"

"Okay, just hear me out," he said. "You don't want another divorce. Right?"

She hesitated before she nodded. "I don't. I want an annulment."

"You have to trust me," he said. "My attorney said that

our best chance at getting an annulment is to wait for Cathy Henderson to get back from vacation."

Sofia looked away and then back at him with a serious expression.

"Okay. So, what do we do in the meantime?"

"I'm glad you asked. I told you that my parents passed away when I was twelve."

"Yes, you did. Again, I'm so sorry, Harris."

"Thank you." He cleared his throat. "But what I'm getting at is that even though my uncle Sander, took my siblings and me in—it was an unconventional upbringing. He's only twelve years older than me. So, in some ways he's more like a brother. Don't get me wrong, I'll always be grateful to him for stepping up for us, but it didn't feel the same as it did when my parents were still alive and we were a traditional family. And because of that, I can't remember what family life—with a mom, dad and kids—is like."

She nodded.

"I'll make a deal with you, if you'll give me ten days while we wait for Cathy Henderson to return. Let me move in with you—we can say I'm an old friend who's visiting—whatever you want. But I want to experience life as a family guy. When the lawyer returns, if you still want out, not only will I agree to the annulment, I'll pay all the expenses, and we can go our separate ways."

He watched her face transform from questioning to horror.

"Are you deranged? There is no way I would ever let a stranger move in with my kids and me."

"Stranger?" he said. "I'm not a stranger."

"Yes, you are. Clearly, you don't understand the dynamics of having kids. Plus, why would I want you hanging around the house for ten days?"

"What if I sleep in that great casita of yours?"

"And what's in this for me except for another mouth to feed and more dishes to wash?"

"Sofia, I would help you. The whole point would be to live together as a family. Except I'll stay in the guesthouse at night, of course."

She stared at him with an impassive expression for what seemed like an eternity.

He didn't blame her for being wary. Emerald Ridge was full of good people, but it also had its fair share of those who acted polite to your face and then turned around and talked about you behind your back.

If the locals got a clue that something was going on between the two of them, she would be the one on whom it would have the biggest impact. That was because he lived in Dallas and was only in and out of Emerald Ridge.

"So if I allow you to live in my guesthouse for two weeks, you'll grant me the annulment without further delay?" she asked.

"Sure, unless you decide you're madly in love with me," he said. "Then we can reopen the discussion."

"Yeah, that's not going to happen. No offense. You know my position, and I'm not changing my mind."

He was so tempted to tell her that he could be very persuasive, but he clamped his mouth shut, determined to let her speak first.

Again, she watched him silently, but he could virtually see the wheels of her mind spinning.

Finally, she said, "Give me the rest of the day to think about it. I'll let you know tomorrow morning."

Chapter Five

After Sofia said goodbye to Harris at the Paris Café, she ditched her errands and went home. Her head was spinning—one minute, she wondered if she had just glimpsed a piece of Harris's heart, and the next, she'd expected him to text and tell her he'd been joking.

I really had you going there, didn't I?

Why would a guy like Harris Fortune want to experience family life with her and her children?

Family life.

It was wonderful, but it was also routine and messy, and full of ups and downs and trying moments that were worth it to her because she loved her children unconditionally.

But what was in it for him?

She wouldn't be telling the truth if she didn't confess that there were times when she was at her wit's end.

More frequently than she'd like to admit.

Kids pushed buttons and boundaries. They tested them and stretched them to the breaking point. That's when she had to put her foot down. Because even though kids pushed, they *needed* limits. That's what made them feel safe and secure, and ultimately grow up to be functioning, law-abiding citizens and loving human beings.

When you loved your kids, it was difficult to enforce those boundaries because who wants to be the bad guy?

But that's what you had to do.

She suspected this was not going to be the picnic that Harris thought he was signing up for.

Was he prepared to argue over bedtimes and deal with dinners when Kaitlin insisted that, *No, she would not eat the icky-looking dinner* because this week she was not eating meat, but she also refused to eat vegetables. How would Harris handle explaining to her daughter why she couldn't subsist on cheese sticks, breaded plant-based dinosaur nuggets and mandarin oranges?

And then there was the staying up all night with a sick child, and school issues, and Jackson being upset at not being able to read yet.

After realizing she'd been pacing around the house like a maniac, she walked out the front door and made her way around to the backyard, and down the brick path overgrown with grass that needed to be mowed, to the guesthouse that was once her studio.

There was a wall of nice French doors off the family room in the main house that overlooked the backyard, but thanks to the humidity and rain, the deck right outside the doors wasn't in the best shape. Before Dan had moved to Austin, he'd been so busy with work and they'd been short on money, which had been the story of their lives it seemed, that fixing the deck hadn't been in the budget. So it had fallen to the bottom of the priority list, and as neglected things go, with each humid day and afternoon thunderstorm, it had fallen into worse and worse repair.

Now, when they wanted to enjoy the backyard—or the casita—they had to exit via the front door, walk around and enter through the gate.

Not ideal, but it was better than someone falling through a rotten board and getting hurt.

Since the school year was well underway and the nights had started turning chillier, the backyard wasn't high on anyone's wish list. But it would be the ideal time to start putting aside a little bit of money each week to have it refurbished in the spring.

That's what she'd do.

Right now, if Harris did take her up on staying in the casita, having to make the extra effort to get inside the house by walking around to the front wasn't necessarily a bad thing.

It was another layer of separation.

But she really would have to do something about the grass. It was much too long. Irritation needled her. Dan had said he'd cut it while she was gone.

He'd been hit-and-miss about keeping the yard neat when he'd lived here. So, it shouldn't have come as a surprise that he hadn't mowed while she was in Las Vegas.

Rather than thinking of it as a passive-aggressive statement, she decided to look at the positive. Mowing would've taken time away from the kids. His love for them was one area where she could never fault him.

As she unlocked the door and stepped inside the little house, she made a mental note to ask the teenager across the street if he wanted to earn a few bucks by mowing.

It had been a while since she'd been out here. It smelled a little musty after being closed up since the spring—the last time they'd had guests stay with them. A guy Dan used to work with at Fortune's Gold Guest Ranch had gotten a job in Michigan. He and his wife had needed a place to stay for a couple of weeks after they'd sold their house earlier than they'd anticipated. So, they'd offered it to them.

Sofia looked around the small space, at the Murphy bed

that they'd installed after she'd opened The Style Lounge downtown to allow for maximum space in the small casita. Continuing her perusal, she assessed the wrought-iron café table and two chairs. The couch and recliner. As well as the tiny kitchenette and the door that led to the compact little bathroom.

Surely, this modest place wouldn't be grand enough for Harris Fortune, who was used to the best of everything. It was barely hospitable enough for weekend guests.

She took a deep breath. The place smelled like another life. One she used to know but didn't belong to her anymore.

Sitting down on the couch, she glanced around the small space once again.

She warred with herself. Maybe if she let Harris stay here, it would be a way to exorcise the past. It would be symbolic of taking back her life and starting over.

Her heart ached at the thought. Not over losing Dan, but of how many years she'd tried her hardest to make their marriage work, only to have it come to this.

But now, it was her life to live the way she wanted.

Within parameters, of course.

And those parameters were her children, which landed her back to square one. Would letting Harris Fortune—a virtual stranger—share ten days of her family's life be the best thing for her children?

Even if she did feel like she knew Harris, she didn't know him. Despite what he'd told her about his unconventional up-bringing, she still didn't understand what he was hoping to gain. What would a man of the world like Harris want with ten days of domestic bliss? In fact, she'd wager that he'd take one look at the casita and he'd backtrack.

Sofia laughed to herself at the thought.

Before she could overthink it any more than she already had, she took out her phone and texted.

Tell me again why you want to move in with my family and me.

A few seconds later, the dots at the bottom of the text page began to dance.

Then they stopped.

And started again.

Was he doing a bit of overthinking himself? Or maybe he didn't know why he wanted to go through with this crazy plan.

Finally, his message popped up.

I want to experience family life.

Her instinct was to send a barrage of question marks, but that would seem rude.

But asking him to further explain over text didn't seem very efficient.

Her gaze darted to the time in the upper left corner of her phone.

She texted back.

My kids will be home in three hours. Do you have time today to come over and look at the casita to see if you really want to spend ten days here? It's not the Four Seasons. I need to leave at 3:30 because I have to pick up my kids.

Harris: I'll be there in ten minutes.

It felt like an eternity, but true to his word, Harris knocked on her front door ten minutes later.

Sofia's heart pounded as she opened the door to greet him. Why was she so nervous?

She *shouldn't* be nervous.

"Hi," she said.

"Hello." A broad smile that made her stomach flip-flop spread over his face. "Long time no see."

She sidestepped him and pulled the door shut behind her. He gave her a quizzical look.

"The casita is around back." As she started walking through the too-long grass, the magnitude of what a bad idea this was hit her. Harris Fortune wouldn't want to live here. Even so, she felt the need to explain.

"Sorry for the grass. I'm between lawn services."

That's right. Just keep it short and sweet. You don't owe him an explanation.

"Sorry to make you walk through it. Some places are called walk-ups. This place is a walk-around."

The corner of his mouth lifted. At least they shared a similar sense of humor.

"No, seriously," she continued. "I need to find someone to fix the steps off the deck. Until I do, when we go into the backyard, we have to walk around."

Stop talking, Sofia. You're making it sound as though you live in ruins.

It wasn't true. He'd just asked to move in at a bad time. She took pride in keeping the inside of the house clean and tidy. In fact, she'd taken a few minutes to dust the casita and turn on the window air-conditioning unit to freshen up the place before he arrived.

It was small. So it hadn't taken long.

As she opened the wooden gate leading to the backyard, she gave herself a mental shake. She wasn't trying to sell him on the property. She reminded herself, as far as she was concerned, he could move in…or not.

He was quiet, which was different for him as he seemed to have an opinion about everything.

She held the gate open for him to pass through and tried to guess what he was thinking…

So, this is how the middle class lives.

Yeah, well, welcome to my world, Fortune.

As she opened the door to the casita, she saw him eyeing the deck.

Judgmental much? Nice.

She shouldn't care what he thought—in fact, it would be better if he decided her humble setup was beneath him. But she was suddenly defensive and protective over the space.

Dan and her cousin had worked hard to build the little wooden-frame house to give her a place to start her business. She'd been so happy then. But that was then and this was now.

One marriage down the tubes and another on deck for annulment.

A heavy sorrow, dark and thick as tar, made her stomach ache.

She opened the door on a blast of cold air and motioned for him to enter.

As she stood in the doorway, she noticed the musty smell was gone. The air conditioner and furniture polish had done the trick.

Harris stood in the middle of the floor and turned in a small circle.

"You are looking at the original Style Lounge, though my salon didn't have a name until I moved to the spot on Emerald Ridge Boulevard. After the move, I had this great little guesthouse."

She laughed for no other reason than to fill the silence.

"It's great," he said.

Unless he was a great actor, he sounded sincere.

"When can I move in?"

His words were bracing. "You really want to move in here?"

He nodded. "Why wouldn't I? I mean, unless there's something wrong with the place. Like a snake infestation. I really don't love snakes. I can deal with them, but I'd prefer not to."

"No. The outside of my property might need a little love, but it's not infested with snakes or anything else." She hadn't meant to sound that edgy.

He grimaced. "I was just joking. I mean, I know you have your hands full with the kids and your business. Frankly, I don't know how you do it all. Let me have a look at your deck. I might be able to fix it. And I can take care of the lawn for you."

"No, you don't have to do that. I know it's not ideal to trudge through long grass, but I want to get some quotes. And the deck is farther down the list. We live on a budget here, Fortune. I—"

The words *I can't afford to fix it right now* lodged in her throat. She was doing the best she could, and she resented having to explain.

So, she wouldn't explain.

"Right. I understand, but let me have a look at it."

"Harris, no. Please."

She reached out to put her hand on his arm, but before they could connect, he was already out the door, walking over to the sagging structure.

Unlike the words that had logjammed in her esophagus, a full-bodied, frustrated groan spilled out for all the world to hear.

All the world except Harris, who seemed oblivious.

Arms crossed, she stood rooted to the spot, away from the deck, on the stepping stones that led from the gate to the casita as he poked and prodded at the sagging wood and peeling paint.

It was humiliating. But she refused to let him see how it affected her.

"It just needs to be shored up a bit. It could use a few new boards and some fresh paint," he said. "The steps need to be replaced. Easy. I can fix it myself for the cost of materials."

She frowned at him.

"Fix it yourself?"

"Did I not tell you I'm a kickass carpenter?" he replied.

"Sorry. You do not strike me as the manual labor type."

"I'm very good with my hands, Sofia."

He'd proven that point in Vegas. She was still having dreams about his hands on her body.

At the thought, all the blood rushed to very private parts that had no business being part of this conversation.

"Seriously," he said. "Let me do it as compensation for moving in here."

Well, okay then. *Compensation.* That worked even better than a bucket of iced water at putting out the fire in her that had started just seconds ago.

"Why are you looking at me like that?" he asked. "I don't intend to move in here without giving you some form of compensation."

She squinted at him. "So you really want to move in? Despite the too-long grass and the dilapidated deck?"

He nodded, and she wasn't sure how she felt.

"Well, we need to set some ground rules," she informed him.

"That's fair. I'll repair the deck and pay for food—"

"Are you saying you want to have meals with my kids and me?"

"Of course, that's part of family life."

She tried to run through the proposal in her head, but her thoughts were jumbled by the idea of seeing Harris every day for ten days. At least she had the wherewithal to say, "I'll agree to that on the condition that you will not mention the marriage or attempt to do anything inappropriate in front of my children."

"Such as?" he asked huskily.

"Don't you dare try to kiss me."

"Oh, so you've been thinking about that, huh?"

The smile on his face was maddening. And sexy, she had to admit.

"Are we talking no kissing just in front of the kids or in private, too?" He pushed.

She bit her bottom lip and tried to shake away thoughts of them making love in Vegas.

"I think you know the answer to that, Harris."

He held her gaze for what seemed like ages before he said, "I'll mow your lawn, too."

"You do not have to do that," she told him.

"I know I don't have to do it, and because you don't expect it, it makes me want to do it all the more."

She wondered if her saying she didn't want him to kiss her fell into that same category of making him want to do it all the more.

"Sounds like we have a deal," he said. "When can I move in?"

On Wednesday, as Harris packed for his stay at Sofia's place, his phone announced an incoming text from his cousin Kelsey. He'd assigned each of his three siblings, Uncle Sander and Kelsey different ringtones so he'd know who was trying to reach him without even looking at the phone.

He and Sofia had agreed that he should arrive at five thirty, so he could meet the kids and they could have dinner together.

He picked up his phone and looked at the message.

Hey, dude, you home?

He was just starting to reply to the text when a knock sounded at his door.

I am. Everything okay?

Pressing Send, he shoved his phone into his back pocket and took the stairs two at a time to answer the door.

It was Kelsey.

"Everything is fine," she said but then pulled a little grimace. "Do you have a minute?"

"For you, always." He and Kelsey were close, more like brother and sister than cousins.

"Always?" she questioned. "Lately, you've been gone more than you've been here. I thought you said you were spending the summer in Emerald Ridge."

"I am, but I still have to work." Though, for the next ten days, he planned on sticking around. He and Sofia hadn't really talked about what they were going to tell people about why he would be hanging around her place so much. Then again, judging from what she'd said, the only people she'd have to explain their living arrangement to would be her kids and Dan, if he came around during that time.

He and his three siblings and Sander and Kelsey didn't keep tabs on each other, but they tried to have the occasional family dinner—usually once a month—so that they could catch up.

They were a tight bunch in their own way. Harris knew it stemmed from losing their parents so young. With Linc Banning's murder, they were all remembering that life was short.

The police were following a lead that involved Linc purchasing adoption records from a former employee of the now-defunct Texas Royale Private Adoption Agency. The police said there were around thirty files that contained the birth names and identified the adoptive families. It was unclear what Linc had planned to do with that information.

If any good had come from this tragedy, it had brought Harris even closer to his siblings.

Even so, he wasn't sure he wanted to tell them about his stay at Sofia's.

Did they really need to know?

"So, I know you've been gone a lot lately, but have you had a chance to search your house for the surprise that your folks left you?" Kelsey asked.

Harris studied her for a moment. "I gave the place a cursory look. I hope you didn't trek all the way over here to ask me that."

Kelsey pulled a face. "Since you hadn't said anything about how it went, someone has to keep you on task. I figured it might as well be me. What exactly does a *cursory look* mean?"

He raised his eyebrows at her. "Um, it means, I didn't take the place apart, but I've looked around to see if there were any obvious hiding places for whatever it is we're looking for."

Kelsey raised her eyebrows back at him. "In other words, you half-assed it."

He laughed.

"If you have time, I'll help you."

"Okay, maybe the search could benefit from another pair of eyes," he said. "I have a thing in about an hour and a half, but if you're up for looking around now, we might as well."

"Where you going tonight?" she asked.

"Nosey," he said, remembering that his suitcase was out and he'd been in the middle of packing.

"Ooh, must be a hot date. You wouldn't be so cagy if it was a business thing or you were meeting friends."

"If you must know, I'm having dinner with a friend."

His cousin's green eyes sparkled. "A *girl* friend?"

"I think we should approach the search strategically," he said, changing the subject with the hopes she'd let the girl-friend inquiry drop. "We might be better off if each of us took a room and looked for places where they might hide something."

"You didn't answer my question." Kelsey's smile was a mile wide. "Does Harry have a girlfriend he hasn't told me about?"

"Is Kelsey thirteen years old? Because she sure is acting like it."

Kelsey laughed and demanded, "Who is she?"

"None of your business."

"Does she live in Emerald Ridge?"

"You take the living room," Harris said, deliberately skirting the subject once again. "And I'll start upstairs. It shouldn't take us long if we get right to work."

That was a strategic move to give him a chance to stash the suitcase before she asked more questions.

A few minutes later, he heard Kelsey's footfalls on the steps, and she appeared on the threshold of his bedroom.

"Any luck?" he asked.

She shook her head. "Without going too crazy or getting too intrusive, I looked in all the likely places downstairs in the living room, dining room and the kitchen, and didn't find any hidden compartments where your folks could've stashed something. That's the good thing about you being such a minimalist, Harry. I didn't have too much to search. I even poked around at the planks of the wooden floor and didn't find anything loose or otherwise questionable. And over the years, you've replaced the furniture, right?"

Harris nodded.

"Do you think the surprise might've been in a piece of the original furniture that was here twenty years ago when they were here?" his cousin asked.

"Do you really think they'd hide anything under a sofa cushion?" Harris asked drolly.

"Your guess is as good as mine," Kelsey replied.

"Let's hope not. I'm pretty sure that my siblings have re-modeled over the years. Let's ask them and see if anyone has hung on to any of the original furniture."

She nodded, but she seemed far away. He got the feeling that she hadn't only come over to help him search.

"So, what's up, Kelsey?"

She blinked. "What do you mean?"

"I don't know," he said. "It seems like you're here but not really here."

She laughed, but there wasn't any humor in the sound.

"You know me too well." Pensively, she bit her bottom lip. "I could use some advice. Do you have time to sit for a minute?"

"Sure. Come on." He brushed past her and motioned with his head for her to follow him downstairs.

He paused at the bottom of the staircase and asked, "Do you want something to drink?"

"No thanks. I'm good. Look, I won't keep you very long since you have somewhere to be."

His gut tightened at the reminder. He glanced at his watch.

He had to finish packing and head toward Sofia's in about an hour. But if his cousin needed him, he wouldn't rush her.

Turning right, he led the way into the living room. He settled into the large, cognac-colored, leather armchair and Kelsey settled on the modern Chesterfield sofa that was covered in deep charcoal velvet.

She looked more fragile than he'd realized earlier and he felt bad for not noticing until now.

"What's up, Kelse?"

She let out a sigh and looked up at the ceiling as if she were either searching for words or steeling herself for something momentous.

Harris let her take her time. Finally, she said, "I'm beginning to wonder if buying The Fortune 8 Ranch was a colossal mistake."

"Why would you say that?"

Granted, she was only twenty-five years old, which was young to take on the responsibilities of a ranch, but his cousin was more mature than most people in their thirties that he knew.

She bit her bottom lip for a moment.

When she didn't answer, he asked, "Are you having buyer's remorse?"

"No," she said almost too quickly. "Well, maybe…but no. You know how long I've wanted to have my own ranch."

It was true. He couldn't remember a time when Kelsey hadn't talked about running her own ranch. After coming into her inheritance, she'd invested wisely. The Fortune 8 was a medium-sized cattle ranch that came complete with a starter herd. It had seemed like a wise choice.

"I know. You've wanted this for a long time. So, what's up? Is it different than what you thought it would be? I know it's hard work."

She leveled him with a death stare. "Since when have I

ever been afraid of hard work? Okay, this is embarrassing to admit, but I'll cut to the chase. I'm having a hard time with the ranch hands."

With her long auburn-red hair and green eyes, his cousin was attractive and had never seemed to have a problem with men—when she wasn't too busy riding herd.

"It's not like that," she said. "The problem is they don't take me seriously. Not only am I having trouble getting them to stay at the ranch, I'm having trouble hiring, too. You're a businessman, Harris. How do I fix this? How do I get them to respect my authority?"

Hmm. That was the last thing he'd expected. Even though she was pretty, she was also somewhat of a tomboy, and that's always the way he'd seen her. It was a part of who she was.

Her mother, Lani Harlow, had been a free spirit who hadn't been able to commit to either Sander or motherhood. So, Sander had agreed to keep her while Lani had gone out to find herself. He'd been confident that if he'd set her free, she'd discover her world was wherever he and their daughter were and come back. Then Lani had died in a car accident in Dallas when Kelsey was just a month old, and Sander had had no choice but to raise her on his own.

She'd grown up around her female cousins Priscilla and Zara, but Kelsey had never really had a mother figure. Raised by her father, Kelsey was used to living in a masculine world. That's why it surprised him that these cowboys had any doubt in her ability.

"What do I do? How do I make them respect me?"

Harris shook his head. "It's your ranch, Kelse. You have to command respect. If they're leaving, then maybe you're better off without them."

"Yeah, but the work doesn't leave with them. It's a lot, and a little overwhelming."

Harris nodded. "Remember that summer when you were about twelve and I tried to spook your horse to get him to buck you off?"

She smirked. "Yeah, that was a real jerk move."

"And you let us know. You put us in our places, and we ended up afraid of you. You need to channel *that* twelve-year-old."

She sighed. "Easier said than done. That twelve-year-old wasn't trying to run a ranch."

"But we didn't mess with you anymore after that. Did we?"

"Well, it was a stupid stunt you pulled," she huffed. "If that horse would've bucked me off, I could've gotten hurt or worse."

Harris pointed at her. "See that conviction, right there?"

Kelsey shrugged.

"Channel *that* attitude. Show the cowboys you won't put up with any crap. You'll have people lining up down to the pasture wanting to work at The Fortune 8 Ranch."

"Good advice." She smiled, but it didn't reach her eyes.

"Kelse, you can do this. You have it in you. You just need to believe you can do it."

With one resolute nod, she said, "I'll think about it."

"Don't think about it," Harris said. "Do it."

He knew that would rile her up, and it did.

"Good talk, cousin." She stood. "I know you have someplace to be. So, I'll get out of your hair. But first, what do you make of that stash of negatives that Priscilla picked up from the photo shop? I don't really know what to make of them."

Harris raked a hand through his hair. "I've been gone so much, I haven't even given them much thought."

"The next time I'm downtown, I'll pop into the frame shop and ask if there are any records of your parents dropping off photographs to frame," she offered.

"That's a good idea," he said. "And I'll talk to Priscilla about the negatives as soon as I get back from Sofia's—" He clamped his mouth shut. He hadn't meant for that to slip out.

Kelsey's mouth fell open and her eyes widened. "So, her name is Sofia? Sofia who?" Her mouth formed a perfect *O*.

"OMG. Are you seeing Sofia Gomez Simon?"

He was too busy mentally kicking himself to answer her. But the knowing look on her face didn't escape him.

"Come on, Harry. I told you *my* secret," she cajoled. "And it's a rather humiliating one at that. Now, you have to tell me yours. Are you and Sofia seeing each other?"

Harris bent forward and straightened a stack of books on the coffee table so that he wouldn't have to look at her, but he knew the cat was out of the bag. At least partially.

"Um. You might say that. It's brand-new and she's wanting to keep things on the down-low until we know where things are going."

It wasn't really a lie. Sofia really did want to keep things quiet. And now Kelsey was standing there looking like he'd just spilled some major tea.

And he had, he supposed.

"Look, Kelse," he said. "I haven't told anyone but you. Can we keep this just between the two of us?"

Kelsey drew a finger and thumb over her lips. "Your secret is safe with me, but, oh my gosh. Marry her, Harry. You two would be the perfect couple, and you'd make such beautiful babies."

Little did his cousin know, he'd already accomplished part of that. Now, his mission for the next ten days was to convince Sofia to remain his lawfully wedded wife.

Chapter Six

At five o'clock sharp, Harris stood on Sofia's front porch, bag in hand, and rang the doorbell.

As he waited, his mind tracked back to Sunday, when he'd dropped her off and her kids had come running out to greet her. He was going to meet those kids now. For a moment, he second-guessed himself and wondered if this was really such a good idea.

Would it work to insert himself into someone else's family? Would he really find what he was looking for?

For a flash, he questioned if he even knew what he was looking for. More of what came next after their night together?

Whatever *next* might be.

As the door opened—for better or worse—he knew he was about to find out.

His smile was automatic, and he worked hard not to let it slip when he realized Sofia wasn't the one at the door, but her little boy... What had she called him on Sunday when she'd asked him to go inside?

Rookie mistake, Fortune. You should've asked her kids' names.

"You were here the other day," said the boy, staring up at him with dark brown eyes that were similar to his mother's.

"Yes. I'm your mommy's friend, Harris Fortune." Harris set down his bag and held out his hand for a shake, but the boy only eyed him in that unabashed way that kids have of staring without shame.

When the boy didn't move, Harris asked, "May I come in?"

He could smell something wonderful cooking, and his stomach growled in appreciation.

"Nope. I'm not supposed to let strangers in the house."

Harris started to ask if that was the case, why was he answering the door, but he bit back the words before they could escape.

"Why do you have a suitcase?"

Unsure what to say because he wasn't sure how much Sofia had told the children, Harris eyed the bag sitting at his feet.

He finally settled on, "I'm going to have dinner with you and fix the deck in your backyard."

The boy seemed unmoved, standing there with one hand on the doorframe and the other on the door, as if weighing whether or not to close the door in Harris's face, relegating him to front porch purgatory.

Then he had an idea. He pulled his phone out of his pocket and texted Sofia.

I'm here, but I can't get past the gatekeeper.

Seconds later, she texted back: ???

He was about to type out an explanation, but he heard Sofia's voice behind her son. "Jackson Carlos, what are you doing?"

The boy turned his head in her direction and said, "This man wants dinner, and he says he's gonna fix our back porch."

"This is my friend, Mr. Fortune. I told you he was coming over," she said. "Step aside and let him in, please."

"Okay." The boy did as he was asked and Sofia appeared behind him, opening the door wider.

Dressed in a black tunic top with a long gold necklace and black leggings, she smiled, and something electric sparked inside Harris's gut.

Her feet were bare, and her toenails were painted bright pink. The color played well against her tanned feet. She was at once casual and elegant.

His mouth was suddenly dry.

"Hi, Harris. Sorry about the gatekeeper." She ruffled the boy's hair and he leaned into her. "Jackson means well, but he can be shy around people he's just met."

"I'm *not* shy, Mommy," the boy said in a stage whisper as he eyed Harris, warily sizing him up.

"Okay, Jackson is not shy," Sofia said. "Go get your sister, please. I want to introduce her to Mr. Fortune."

The boy galloped off, calling, "Kaitlin! Mommy wants you to meet Mr. Fortune."

"Mr. Fortune? That's so formal. Would you mind if they called me Harris?"

Sofia tilted her head back and looked up at him as if contemplating her answer. Finally, she said, "Normally, I have them address adults by their surname as a show of respect. What if they called you Mr. Harris?"

Jackson and Kaitlin came running up and skidded to a stop next to their mother. The dark-haired girl looked like Sofia's mini-me. She slid her hand into her mother's as she gazed up at Harris.

"Kaitlin Maria, this is Mr. Fortune. He is a friend of mine. He just told me that you and Jackson can call him Mr. Harris. Harris is his first name. Harris, this is my daughter, Kaitlin Maria."

"Mommy calls me Kaitlin Maria, but you can just call me Kaitlin." The girl smiled, and Harris noticed she was missing her two front teeth, which was adorable.

"Nice to meet you, Kaitlin," Harris said.

"Come in," Sofia told him. "Make yourself at home. Dinner should be ready in about fifteen minutes. Kids, is your homework finished?"

"Mine is!" Kaitlin raised her hand and hopped up and down a little bit. "But Jackson still hasn't finished his reading worksheet. He played with the salt and pepper shakers instead of doing his homework. Can I watch the kids' baking show?"

"Yes, for a few minutes while I get dinner on the table," Sofia said. "Let's go into the family room and I'll turn on the television for you."

"We're not allowed to turn on the TV until we finish our homework," Kaitlin informed Harris as she hopped up and down a few more times before skipping off ahead of them. Jackson raced ahead, too.

Sofia paused and motioned to Harris's bag, which he'd set to the left of the door. "Would you like to take that out to the casita and get settled in while I finish dinner prep?"

"No, I'd like to help you," he said. "I set a mean table."

"You're telling me you have skills, huh?"

Sofia glanced in the direction that the kids had gone. Harris followed her gaze. They were out of hearing range.

"I have mad skills. You have no idea."

Sofia quirked a brow. "Yeah, well, just remember our agreement."

He wanted to push the boundaries a little. After all, she'd started it when she'd said the bit about him having skills, but she was already walking away.

As Harris followed her out of the foyer, he glanced around, drinking in everything as they walked past formal dining and living rooms, a staircase with dark wooden treads and handrail separated by white spindles. A classic-looking Persian runner ran up the stairs, secured in place by brass rods at the base of the risers.

To be honest, he hadn't been sure what to expect since the grass had been long and the deck was in such a state that she had deemed it unsafe.

The inside of the house, with its sophisticated air, was more in line with what he'd come to associate with Sofia. They walked into an open-concept kitchen and family room that looked a lot more lived-in than the first rooms he'd passed on the way in.

With pots and pans in the sink and on the counters, the kitchen was definitely a workshop of good things.

"Something smells wonderful," Harris said, inhaling a deep breath of something that smelled deliciously tomatoey and garlicy.

"I hope you like lasagna," Sofia murmured.

"I do. In fact, it's one of my favorites."

"Is there meat in the lasagna?" Kaitlin made a face and flung herself onto an overstuffed sofa as her mother turned on the television.

"It's the same lasagna I always make," Sofia said. "You love my lasagna, Kaitlin."

Her daughter didn't answer. Instead, she stared at the TV, where a girl who looked about her age detailed the virtues of fondant versus frosting. It was fascinating that someone so young had even heard of fondant.

Sofia announced, "Kids, five minutes until dinner." She turned to Harris. "Would you please fill the water glasses while I dish up the plates?"

"Happy to."

"Normally, I wouldn't turn on the television this close to dinner," she said. "But I thought it might settle them down before we sit down to eat."

Harris held up his hands. "No judgment here. Seems educational. I'm dying to know the difference between fondant versus frosting. What is fondant, anyway?"

"It's a type of cake icing that's way too sweet for me."

He was thinking about how sweet her lips had tasted and that he had a sudden craving to savor them again when their gazes met. Something electric passed between them. Harris knew she felt it, too, but she pointed toward the fridge and turned away.

"The glasses are in the cabinet, and the water is in the door of the refrigerator."

By the time Harris filled the glasses with ice and water and got them on the table, Sofia had set full plates at each place setting and was calling the kids to the table.

They had just gotten settled in when Harris glanced at Jackson in time to see him shovel a large bite of lasagna into his mouth and stick out his tongue at his sister.

"Eww! Mommy, tell Jackson to stop showing me his food. It's gross."

"Jackson Carlos, stop it," Sofia said. "What did we talk about recently?"

The boy smiled a goofy grin, shrugged and tilted his head to the side so that his cheek nearly rested on his left shoulder. He raised his fork, which was in his right hand.

"Would you like to be excused?" Sofia's tone made it clear she wasn't playing.

"I would," Kaitlin said.

Sofia glanced at the girl's full plate. "You have not touched your meal, young lady."

"I don't eat meat or anything green."

"Okay, we're not doing this tonight," Sofia said. "I worked hard to make dinner for you and…"

"Eww," Jackson said through a mouthful of lasagna and

pushed his plate away. "I don't eat meat or green things either."

He crossed his arms in solidarity with his sister.

"Jackson Carlos Simons, do not talk with your mouth full," Sofia scolded. "I will not tell you again."

The boy slumped back into his chair. His bottom lip protruded. There was a ring of marinara sauce around his pouting mouth.

An awkward silence fell over the room.

"Wow, this broccoli tastes really good," Harris said to Sofia. "I think it must be special broccoli. Is it special?"

He took another bite, and as he chewed, he set down his fork, crossed one forearm atop the other in front of his chest and flexed. "Did you see that? This is definitely special broccoli because I just felt myself get stronger, which is a good thing because I need all the strength I can get to do those repairs on the deck."

The boy was watching him.

"Jackson, feel that muscle." Harris pointed to his bicep. "I just got one hundred percent stronger from eating that broccoli. Do you feel it?"

The boy nodded, a look of wonder in his eyes.

"So, buddy, if you're not going to eat your broccoli, I'd love to have it because I need to be extra strong to get all that work done."

The boy ducked his head and poked at the broccoli on his plate with his fork. For a moment Harris feared the plan might backfire and Jackson might give him the vegetable.

"Do you know how to build things like tree houses?" he asked.

"You bet I do," Harris replied. "Why? Do you want one?"

The boy's mouth fell open and he nodded fiercely.

"I don't think so," Sofia interjected.

Harris gestured to the stem of broccoli on his plate. "Did you ever notice how broccoli looks like little trees?"

Both kids looked at their plates and then nodded.

"Only kids who eat broccoli can have tree houses, because it takes a lot of strength to climb all the way up the ladder into the tree house." He shrugged. "I wish I could help you out because I build really good tree houses, but if you don't like broccoli…" Harris pulled a frown and shrugged again, then looked around. "Don't tell anyone I told you this, but broccoli is the secret food of all tree house owners. You've gotta like broccoli to have a tree house."

Harris felt Sofia's gaze on him, but he kept his eyes on Jackson, who had speared his broccoli and shoved as much as he could into his mouth.

"If he gets a tree house, I want a balance beam," Kaitlin declared. "I'm really good at gymnastics. I just started taking lessons at the Emerald Ridge gymnasium. Want to see my cartwheel?"

Kaitlin pushed back from the table, the chair's legs screeching on the tile floor.

"Cartwheels are for the outside, young lady," Sofia said. But the girl was already up and hopping around before presenting a pretend balance beam routine, arms outstretched, putting one small sock-clad foot in front of the other and performing a teetering pirouette.

"You like gymnastics?" Harris asked.

"Yes." She pirouetted again in a tiny circle.

Harris asked the girl if she'd heard of Simone Biles, the Olympic gymnastics gold medalist.

Kaitlin nodded enthusiastically. "I have a poster of her in my bedroom. I want to do gymnastics in the Olympics when I grow up."

"Did you know that most Olympic gymnasts love broccoli

because it makes them strong? Just like I said before." Harris flexed. "And look at your brother. Look how much stronger he is already after only eating one broccoli tree."

Jackson sprang up from the table, flexed his arms out to the side and roared. "I am very strong. I'm as strong as a big tree."

"I guess since you love broccoli, now I have to build you a tree house," Harris told him.

"Harris…" Sofia said.

Kaitlin slid back into her chair. "If I eat my broccoli, will I get a balance beam?"

Before Harris could answer, Kaitlin had speared the vegetable and was munching on the florets.

After she'd finished, she pointed at her plate. "See, I ate all my broccoli, and I didn't hate it."

"I like broccoli, too," Jackson said. "Look how big and strong I am."

Harris braved a glance at Sofia, who was shaking her head as she cradled it in her hand.

"Well then, I guess I have no choice but to build one tree house and one balance beam."

The kids ran out of the room cheering.

"Please tell me you did not just offer to build a tree house and a balance beam for my children without asking me first," Sofia said.

"Okay, I won't tell you unless you ask." He sounded genuinely contrite. "And I'm sorry. I didn't mean to disrespect your authority."

"Harris, no. I have to put my foot down." Fortunately, she didn't sound as mom-scary as she had when she'd reminded her children of their manners.

"Before you tell me it's not in the budget, I offered, so it's on me."

"No," she said.

At an impasse, they stared at each other until Harris finally said, "Well, then you'll have to be the one who disappoints them."

"Well, they'll get over it. One of the hardest lessons in life is that you don't get everything you want."

"I know that," he said. "I never had a tree house when I was Jackson's age."

He shrugged, and he saw her expression soften.

"You can't just offer my children gifts without asking me first."

"I'm sorry. From now on, I promise to follow the chain of command. But every boy needs a tree house, Sofia. Plus, I got them to eat their broccoli."

She sighed. "Every child does *not* need a treehouse. You didn't have one and you survived. Plus, I can't have them thinking they'll get something in exchange for doing things they should do automatically."

"They're kids. Hating broccoli is a rite of passage," he reminded her.

Their gazes locked in a standoff.

Finally, she sighed. It sounded like the weight of the world was contained in that one exhalation.

"If there are any broken bones, you're responsible," she said. "Even though you think you won the first parenthood test, you actually failed. So, don't be too proud of yourself."

Then a wicked look flashed in her eyes. "Oh, and by the way, while we're on the subject of parenting, my cousin Jacinta is ill this week, and Abuela Rosa is running the shop while Jacinta is out. My parents are living the dream in LA, which means they are permanently out of pocket. The school has a new policy where we have to provide alternative contacts if the ones we list are unavailable. So, you want a taste of family life, Fortune? I'm putting you down as a contact. I'll print the form you need to fill out."

"I'm happy to be on the contact list," he said. "We are married after all. Technically, that makes me their stepfather."

"Shhhhh!" Her finger flew to her lips. "Shush!"

She looked around for the kids and gave him an exasperated palms-up gesture.

"Relax, they can't hear us."

"One of the basic rules in Parenting 101 is little ears hear everything. Especially when they're not in the room and you're saying something you don't want them to hear."

She smiled and started to give him a playful punch on the arm, but he caught her hand in his and pulled her closer. Their gazes locked, and that feeling that had passed between them earlier sizzled again, but then he heard the sound of kids squabbling in the other room. Sofia pulled away, stood and started grabbing dinner dishes off the table.

"I'll wash, you dry?" she said.

Great.

Thanks to Harris's handing out tree houses and balance beams like Santa Claus, Jackson and Kaitlin had stars in their eyes for him.

Sofia grimaced as she washed the last bowl and handed it to Harris to dry.

She should have made one of the ground rules that he was not allowed to barge in here and endear himself to her children.

As Harris chatted away about his family and why they'd all decided to stay in Emerald Ridge for the summer—something about searching for a present that their late parents had left them before they died—Sofia's thoughts kept drifting back to how Kaitlin and Jackson had taken to Harris.

But what was the alternative? She certainly didn't want her children to hate this man who was staying with them for the next week-and-a-half. But what would happen if they got attached to him and he left?

They were still coming to terms with the divorce and that their father no longer lived with them…

Sofia gave herself a mental shake. This was a no-win situation, and it was making her feel a little stabby.

She thought he would've been overwhelmed by being added to the emergency call list. So, yes, it was a test—or maybe not a test, as much as a *You want a taste of family life? Buckle up, buster, I'll show you.*

He hadn't batted an eye. Similarly, the kids' mealtime antics hadn't made him shrink away.

Sighing, she pulled a clean kitchen towel out of the drawer and dried her hands on it.

"Bedtime is at 8:00 p.m. I need to help the kids with their routine so they can start winding down. Feel free to retire to the casita."

"And miss story time?" He smiled, and when she didn't respond, he added, "I don't want to intrude. Thank you for the delicious meal and for…this."

He made an all-encompassing gesture that she took to mean the *living situation*.

As he turned to walk away, she heard herself saying, "You can stay for story time as long as you're willing to be the reader. It's an important part of the bedtime ritual and the bedtime ritual is one of the pillars of family life. So, if you're game, you're welcome to join in."

What she had conveniently left out was that bedtime often included an overly tired Kaitlin getting upset because she wanted to hear *another* installment of the chapter book they were reading or she wanted to try her hand at reading it. Or how Jackson was prone to getting one last burst of energy and zooming up and down the hallway only to return and leap onto his sister's bed where he would give his best recitation of the poem, *Five Little Monkeys Jumping on the Bed*, jumping higher and getting louder over his sister's screams of protests. Sometimes, Kaitlin would think it was funny and laugh, but lately, she got upset.

Sometimes, the two would be in cahoots—like the night they'd decided they were cats and crawled under the bed and refused to come out. Sofia had ended up turning off the light and walking out of the room, but Jackson, who sometimes was afraid of the dark, had bumped his head on the bed frame as he'd tried to crawl out and cried for a half hour.

Sofia smiled to herself, wondering how this single man who hadn't a clue about raising children would handle something like that.

We'll see.

"Is there anything I can do to help while you get the kids ready for bed?"

She almost said no but then thought better of it.

"How do you feel about packing school lunches?"

He raised his brows. "*Um*, what exactly does that entail?"

"Oh no, never mind. I can do it after I get the kids down."

"No, please, I'd really like to help you."

She felt herself slipping into her *It's easier to do it myself* mode, but stopped short. "Tomorrow, they can have peanut butter and jelly. You'll find some baby carrots in the fridge's vegetable bin, and there are pretzels in the pantry. You'll find zip lock bags in there, too. Lunch boxes are on the counter. But you'll need to clean them out and give them a good wipe-down and—"

He held up his hand to stop her. "It's fine. I'm sure I can figure it out."

She was opening her mouth to ask him if he really would've known to clean the lunch boxes, but at the last second, she realized it might've sounded a little insulting. Or condescending, at the very least.

She could always check the lunch boxes. If he didn't do it right, she could do it over after he went out to the casita.

"Okay, family man. Have at it."

She turned to go but stopped and looked back. "Thank you, Harris. I appreciate the help."

She blew out a breath as she walked away. She did appreciate it… Despite the fact that letting someone else shoulder some of the load where the kids were concerned made her feel vulnerable, off-kilter, and strangely out of her element. Maybe while Harris was here playing house, she'd learn how to be better at delegating.

If he lasts that long.

She chuckled to herself.

Forty-five minutes later, she came downstairs and found Harris sitting on the family room couch, reading something on his phone. He'd straightened up the room. Not obsessively so, just grouping toys and lining up shoes along the wall.

"Looks nice in here." She smiled at him. "Are you one of those people who has to have everything in its place?"

He grinned back at her and stood. "And what if I am?"

"Then you're going to be in for a wild ride, Fortune. Just saying. The kiddos are snug in their beds and ready for their bedtime stories. Still up for it?"

"Of course," he said.

As she motioned for him to follow her upstairs, she started to say, *Don't let their adorableness fool you.* But then it hit her that even though she thought her kids were adorable—no, she *knew* they were—he might not agree. If that was the case, she'd have to kick him out. Plus, it would be much more fun to watch him be taken in by them and then taken by surprise when the little monkeys sprang into action.

They alternated weeks for whose room hosted the nightly story. This was Kaitlin's week, and Jackson was already waiting with his sister in her room.

"Kids, Mr. Harris would like to read to you tonight," Sofia said. "Is that okay?"

Cheers went up in the bedroom.

"Okay, settle down," she said as Harris dragged Kaitlin's little pink-and-white desk chair over to the side of the bed.

"Is this alright?" Harris asked.

The kids nodded.

"Absolutely," Sofia said, a little taken aback for not having thought out the bedtime-story logistics herself. Of course, it would be awkward for him to snuggle in the bed like the kids were used to doing with her. She wouldn't have wanted him to do that anyway. And because he respected the boundaries, she suddenly felt better about having him around.

"What book are we reading?" Harris asked.

Seeing his large frame spilling over the child-sized chair made Sofia smile.

"Happy Tales From the Enchanted Forest." Kaitlin presented the book to him, and he took it. "We're on chapter four. It's where the bookmark is."

Sofia watched Harris open the book and give it a cursory glance before he jumped in...with both feet. She was impressed by the heart and soul he put into the effort. He used different voices for the forest animals, and soon he had the kids hanging on his every word. Their big brown eyes grew large, and they leaned in when Harris would emphasize something in the story. He had the good sense to slowly bring the energy down as he went along—never losing the integrity of the tale—and by the time he'd reached the end of the chapter, Kaitlin was looking very sleepy and Jackson was sound asleep.

Harris was…good at this. *Really good.*

He picked up the little boy and Sofia showed him the way to Jackson's room, where he laid down her son and tucked him in as if Jackson were his own.

When they returned to Kaitlin's room, however, the little girl was sitting up with her feet dangling over the side of the bed.

"Mommy, I'm supposed to bring cupcakes to school tomorrow."

Sofia's mouth fell open. "And why are you telling me this *now*? How long have you known about this?"

"I told Daddy when he was here," she said.

"Kaitlin Maria, your father was here this weekend. He's not the one providing the cupcakes. It's almost eight o'clock. I'm not sure I have all the ingredients to whip up a batch tonight—" She stopped midsentence because she could hear the pitch of her voice rising.

"I'm sorry," Kaitlin sobbed, and a tear ran down her cheek.

"What time do you have to be at school in the morning?" Harris asked. He was standing behind her, and for a moment, she'd forgotten he was there. This was karma coming back to bite her since she'd wished he would experience a dose of real life as a family.

"Eight o'clock," Kaitlin said. "We always leave here twenty minutes early, so we're not late."

"No sweat," he said. "The ER Grocery opens at seven o'clock. I'll be there when they open and get back before you have to leave. How does that sound?"

Kaitlin smiled through her tears. "That sounds good."

"Can you say thank you to Mr. Harris?"

"Thank you, Mr. Harris."

"You're very welcome. Now get a good night's sleep and don't worry about a thing, okay?"

She smiled and nodded, and laid her head on her pillow. Sofia's heart was overflowing as she pulled the covers up and tucked her little girl in.

"I love you, Mommy."

Sofia smoothed Kaitlin's hair off her forehead. "I love you, too, *mija*. Now, go to sleep."

Maybe having some help wasn't the worst thing in the world. In fact, it was kind of nice.

Once they were downstairs, Sofia said, "Thank you, Harris."

"For what?"

She flashed what she hoped was her best sardonic smile. "False modesty is not a good look, Fortune."

Constantly being defensive probably didn't look very good on her either.

As she walked toward the front door, an unspoken hint for Harris to follow, she remarked, "You seem like a natural when it comes to parenting."

"I don't know about that," he said. "But Kaitlin and Jackson are great kids. They made it easy."

She couldn't stop pride from turning up the corners of her mouth.

Pausing at the front door, she put her hand on the knob but didn't open it.

"Thanks for offering to pick up the cupcakes in the morning. Are you sure it's not too much trouble? If it is, I can swing by the store on the way to school."

"I'll be up early anyway," he replied. "I'm happy to help you any way I can while I'm here."

While I'm here.

Tonight had gone a lot better than she'd thought it would.

She'd thought it would be awkward. No, actually, she'd feared tonight would be downright *painful*. She had this walking nightmare in which Harris realized middle-class family life was boring. He'd get quietly impatient with the kids and end up cutting the visit short.

If she was completely honest with herself, she'd hoped that's how it would turn out.

She'd been wrong.

Because the truth was, she kind of liked having him here.

Sofia opened her mouth to tell him she'd be right back. That she needed to get some money from her purse for the cupcakes. But what she really needed was to step away for a minute and put some space between them.

She stopped short. Staring up at him in the dim light of the foyer, seeing how the light and shadows played off his handsome face—turning his green eyes to deep jade, accentuating his strong jawline and that nose that looked like it might have been broken once, and those lips that had kissed her in front of the Vegas Eiffel Tower...

All of that was enough to render her speechless, but it was the way he was looking back at her that took her breath away.

She'd only meant to lean in and hug him—a chaste goodnight, a gesture of gratitude—but then the next thing she knew, her lips were on his and she was kissing him like she never wanted him to leave.

Chapter Seven

The next morning, grocery bag in hand, Harris carefully traversed the deck's dilapidated steps and decided to test the platform before putting his full weight on it. He toed a board with his loafer then pressed down on it with his foot, assessing it. Despite the peeling barn-red paint and rotting and missing boards toward the middle, this spot seemed safe enough. He walked to the house's French doors but was stopped by a flash of movement through the kitchen window.

Sofia was at the stove, stirring something. She wore an apron over her clothes. *What a beautiful woman.* He stood rapt, watching her for a moment and remembering the kiss they'd shared last night.

The memory of her lips on his—how she'd tasted of honey and sunshine and promise—made his heart squeeze and longing unfurl in his gut.

Last night, the way she'd leaned in and kissed him good-night had just about made him come undone. All he knew as he stood there this morning was that he wanted more.

He shifted the brown paper bag to his left hip and rapped on the kitchen window with his knuckle. Sofia jumped and whirled around, holding the spatula like a weapon.

Harris waved. She blinked a couple of times before the fiercely protective look on her face morphed into one of confusion, then concern. She moved the pan from the burner, set down the utensil on a spoon holder and motioned to the right.

Harris met her at the French doors.

"Good morning," he said after she opened the door.

He was just about to lean in for another kiss when she asked, "What are you doing, Harris? You startled me."

"I come bearing cupcakes." He held out the grocery sack as if it was his ticket for admittance. She accepted it, peering inside, and murmured, "Thank you for picking these up, but what I meant was, why are you on the deck? It's not safe. You could've fallen through and gotten hurt."

She stepped back and motioned for him to enter. He did and they stood next to the table where they'd eaten dinner last night. This morning, it was set for three, complete with buttered whole-wheat toast and small glasses of orange juice. Clearly, she wasn't expecting him for breakfast. That was okay. She didn't have to provide every meal.

"I hate to break it to you," he said. "I will have to get in the middle of it while I'm repairing the deck. For the most part, it appears to be structurally sound. It just needs some shoring up."

"You should've come to the front door rather than risking hurting yourself."

"I didn't want to use the front door." He bit off the words like tough bites of meat.

Sofia raised her brows at him. "What's wrong with my front door?"

"There's nothing wrong with your front door. It feels like knocking on the front door defeats the purpose of this... This...*experiment* that we're doing."

Plus, he'd used the front door when he'd arrived, and now that he was living here—there was already enough distance between them without his having to walk around to the front of the house and knock on the door like a stranger every time he wanted her to let him in.

Her face folded into a frown. *"Right. Our Great Experiment."* She glanced over her shoulder as if she was looking for someone. Then she met his eyes and lowered her voice to just above a whisper. "Well, let me make something perfectly clear. There will be no more kissing in this experiment. I am not your lab rat, Fortune."

He couldn't hold back the laugh that escaped. "Lab rat?"

"You know what I mean," she mumbled.

"Hold on a second," he said. *"You* kissed *me.* And I have to be honest, I didn't hate it."

She pressed her index finger to her lips and hissed, *"Shhhhhhh!* Little kids have big ears. We'll talk about this later. Sit down, and I'll get your breakfast."

"You don't have to fix my breakfast," he said.

"I already did. It's the least I can do to thank you for picking up the cupcakes this morning. By the way, how much do I owe you?"

He waved off her question. "Nothing. I got it."

"No, I want to repay you. I meant to give you some money last night, but—"

Her eyes flashed, and she clamped her mouth shut.

He quirked a brow suggestively because he knew she was going to say something about the kiss and getting flustered before she'd basically shoved him out the front door.

"I know," he said. "I'm that hard to resist."

She actually sputtered before finding her words. "Sit down and stop talking about… *That.* No, wait. Would you please go to the base of the stairs and holler up to the kids that breakfast is ready."

He smiled. "Hollering is allowed in this house? You struck me as someone who wouldn't love that."

"No. Usually, it is not," she enunciated. "This morning, I'm making a special exception. Please tell the kids that breakfast is ready. And, Harris, not another word about last night. Okay?"

He shrugged and smiled again, implying that he'd think about it. But, of course, he wasn't going to talk in front of the kids about kissing their mother because he really wanted to kiss her again.

And he didn't want to ruin his chances of that happening.

"You're right," he said. "Before there's any talk of kissing, we really should tell them that it's okay because we're married."

Her mouth fell open and she raised her hands to the side of her face, shaking them as if she wasn't sure if she wanted to cover her face or reach out and strangle him.

"I'll get the kids," he told her. "Be right back." He turned and walked to the foot of the staircase, where he called for the kids to come down for breakfast.

His joking front had masked confusion. He'd been prepared to play by the rules that she'd set. Then she'd turned those rules on their head.

Now, he wasn't sure which way was up.

It would help if he wasn't so damned attracted to her.

As he waited for the kids, he mulled over the situation. It wasn't just attraction he felt for her, but he couldn't readily identify that *other* feeling.

He'd been attracted to plenty of women in his lifetime, but none had captured him the way Sofia had. That's the reason those relationships hadn't lasted. While he'd cared about all of them, he hadn't been compelled to fight for them to remain in his life the way he was for Sofia.

Not since Amanda.

He knew how that had ended, and it added another wrinkle

of complication to the Sofia situation. When he factored in how blindsided he'd been by Amanda, he almost wanted to give Sofia the annulment she so desperately wanted.

But something stopped him.

Digging down deep, he knew their chances for an annulment were slim, and he wondered if it was the fact that he didn't want his first marriage to end in divorce that made him keen on making this work. He knew that was at least partially true, but before he could work out the rest of the equation, Kaitlin and Jackson came bounding down the stairs.

Kaitlin was holding on to the banister with her left hand. She held her right hand high above her head.

"It's mine," Jackson yelled. "Give it back!" The boy wasn't as tall as his older sister. Even though he had the advantage of being on the step behind her, he still couldn't match her reach. But that didn't stop him from jumping up as he descended the stairs, trying to get whatever it was Kaitlin held in her hand.

Harris's heart nearly stopped as he imagined the boy falling forward and tumbling down the stairs, taking his sister with him. He forced himself to keep his arms down by his sides, but was at the ready to spring into action if the kids tumbled.

"Hey, careful, guys! Kaitlin, please slow down. Jackson, please hold on to the handrail."

To his surprise, they listened to him. Kaitlin, who now was at the bottom of the steps, held her closed fist across her chest as if getting ready to say the pledge of allegiance.

"Good morning," he said. "What's the problem here?"

"She's got my spider!" Jackson wailed. "Give me back my spider."

"I'm sure we can figure this out," Harris said. "Kaitlin, do you have his spider?"

The girl opened her palm and held it out to reveal a tarantula. For a second before Harris realized it was made of rubber, it made him flinch.

"Jackson keeps trying to scare me by putting this in my bed." Her voice was matter-of-fact and sounded so much older than her seven years. "I told him the next time he did that I was keeping it."

She clamped her fist shut again, tossed her long dark hair and marched in the direction of the kitchen. At that moment, she looked like a miniature version of her mother and it was hard for Harris to suppress a smile. So he rubbed his hand over his mouth in what he hoped was a thoughtful gesture as he looked at Jackson, who was standing there with his little arms hanging down by his sides and a big scowl pinching his face.

Harris motioned to the stairs with a jerk of his head before he sat down on the second step. The boy sat next to him and hunched over.

"Am I in trouble?" he asked.

"You're not in trouble with me, buddy," Harris said. "But you might want to talk to your sister about things. She didn't seem very happy."

Jackson laughed quietly. "It's really funny when she finds it. I've done it like a million times. I can't believe she still gets scared."

"Yeah, some people don't love spiders as much as you seem to."

The boy shrugged.

"I know sometimes it can seem kind of funny to pull pranks like that," Harris continued. "I have two sisters and I used to love to do things like that. But soon I realized that it was more important for me to get along with them. And you know what happened after that?"

"What?" Jackson asked.

"We became friends. You two seem like you could be pretty good friends, too. If I were you, I'd talk to her about it. You might even tell her you don't mean to scare her. Just a suggestion, but talking things out when there's a problem is always a good way to go." He ruffled the kid's hair. "Well, we'd better get in there for breakfast before your mom comes looking for us."

When they got to the kitchen, he saw that Sofia had set a place for him. There were four glasses of orange juice and plates of bacon and eggs on the table.

Harris sat down in the chair next to Sofia's—the same spot he'd sat last night for dinner—and picked up the coffee mug she'd set at his place.

"You really didn't have to do this," Harris said, "but I do appreciate it. I'm starving."

"I wasn't sure how you took your coffee." She looked down at her plate, a hint of pink blooming on her smooth cheeks. Harris wondered if she was thinking the same thing that he was—that they were married, yet they didn't know many intimate things about each other. Like how they each took their coffee. "There's half-and-half and sugar in the kitchen if you want it."

"No, this is perfect. I take it black. You make a good cup of Joe."

She looked at him, and something unspoken and meaningful passed between them.

"I'm sorry I put the spider in your bed," Jackson said to his sister, breaking the spell.

"Jackson Carlos, what did I—"

He hadn't meant to interfere, but instinct made him reach out and grab her hand, which was resting on her lap under the table.

She stopped and looked at him, and he gave an almost imperceptible nod toward Jackson, who was saying, "Mr. Harris, told me I should talk to you about it so you wouldn't be mad at me anymore. So, since I talked to you and said sorry, can I have my spider back?"

Kaitlin lifted her chin—a gesture Harris realized he'd seen Sofia make dozens of times—and said, "I'll think about it."

After breakfast, Harris helped them carry cupcakes and backpacks out to the car. When the kids were inside the car, he noticed Kaitlin had returned the spider to her brother.

Holding Sofia's gaze, he gestured toward the kids. "Talking about things never hurts."

Sofia paused, her hand on the driver's-side door. "So I see."

"Have lunch with me today," Harris said. "I'll pick up something for us to eat. You could meet me here. And we could talk. About things."

The interior of The Style Lounge was a sleek blend of modern luxury and elegance. The soft lavender walls were meant to create a calming backdrop that encouraged clients to relax, while accents of deep, rich aubergine and sleek, glossy black provided a sense of sophistication and class. The oversized silver-framed mirrors at every styling station reflected the light streaming in from Emerald Ridge Boulevard and the chandeliers hanging from the salon's ceiling.

The place felt expansive and expensive.

Usually, it was Sofia's sanctuary.

Not today.

She'd dropped the kids off at school and had been at the salon for a couple of hours. By now, she thought she'd have her thoughts sorted and her feelings under control, but she was still a bundle of nerves.

More like a live wire.

She kept trying to convince herself that she didn't want

to kiss Harris again, but no matter how many times she told herself that, she knew it wasn't true.

The steady hum of the blow dryer filled the air as she lifted and smoothed sections of her client Billie Monroe's blond bob with a round brush. Sofia watched the strands fall into place, silky and smooth. There was something therapeutic about it, something grounding.

She tried to focus on the white noise, on the simple rhythm of the task, and not on what she and Harris might talk about at lunch.

But even the loudest blow dryer couldn't drown out the accusatory voice reminding her that she had changed the rules on Harris. She hadn't meant to, but she hadn't been able to help herself last night. One moment, they were standing in the foyer, and the next, they were…*she was*…kissing him.

Her stomach somersaulted at the memory, causing her to draw in a quick breath. Sofia's hand stilled for a moment as she tried to will the butterflies back into their box.

She glanced at the huge silver clock on the salon wall. It was 11:20. She had a two-hour break between clients after she finished with Billie, but until then, she needed to focus on what she was doing.

Sofia resumed the rhythmic motion of lifting and smoothing, but once again her mind wandered like a stray cat.

When she'd laid out the rules before Harris had moved into the casita—no romantic touches, no kisses, no talk of the marriage—he hadn't argued. He'd respected her boundaries, which she'd set to protect her children…and herself.

Sofia gently turned Billie's head to the side, the strands of hair falling perfectly into place as she continued to dry her locks.

That kiss.

It had been all her. She'd own it.

Harris had read to the kids and tucked them in with such tenderness that it had caught her off guard. Her defenses were already down. Then he'd offered to pick up the cupcakes, which was the equivalent of a white knight riding to the rescue.

And she prided herself on not needing rescuing.

A reflex developed while she was married because…self-preservation. Dan had never been that chivalrous.

Or maybe it was that he'd become comfortable. Why put himself out when he knew Sofia would do it?

Still, there was something in Harris's selfless gesture that made her defenses fall away. And she'd kissed him, breaking her own rules, because in that moment, she'd seen him not just as the man she'd accidentally married but as someone who seemed good for her and her kids.

Someone who *cared*.

Truthfully, last night, she hadn't thought about it that hard. She'd been running on primal instinct.

Now, she was nervous about meeting him for lunch. They'd be alone, and she wasn't entirely sure she could trust herself.

Suddenly, she didn't want to.

Maybe.

Ugh.

What if her mixed signals, her pulling him close only to push him away—and the reality of what *family life* entailed had scared him off?

Sofia's stomach twisted. Because whether this was right or wrong, she honestly didn't want him to go.

She turned off the blow dryer, setting it on the counter as she smiled at Billie's reflection in the mirror.

"How's that?" she asked, brushing a few stray locks of hair off the client's shoulder.

"Perfect, as always," Billie said with a satisfied smile.

As she walked her client to the front of the salon, their heels clicking on the polished black-marble floors, her heart beat a little faster. She wasn't sure what Harris was going to say when they met for lunch, but for the first time, she knew what she wanted. She wanted to see if this thing between them could actually work.

At least she wanted to try.

But try *what*?

Harris had called it an experiment, which sounded ephemeral. She certainly didn't want to get emotionally involved in an experiment that was bound to end.

What should she tell him? That she was wrong to kiss him and they should keep the rules as they were…or should they negotiate a change?

Sofia pondered the questions while touching up her makeup in the mirror at her station but was startled back to the present by the sound of her ringing phone.

She grabbed her cell from her purse and saw a picture of her abuela's face smiling at her from the lock screen.

"*Hola, abuela.* Is everything okay?"

"*Hola, mi amada. Sí.* Everything is fine. In fact, it couldn't be better. I just received the most wonderful news."

"Really?" Sofia murmured. "Do tell."

"My best friend from school, Connie, will be in town on Monday. She will be passing through on her way to visit her family in Florida, and she has made time to see me. We keep in touch, but it's been decades since we've seen each other." Abuela sounded so happy. "I am as giddy as a schoolgirl over the thought of seeing her. *Mija*, I don't mean to impose on you, but my place is too small to host her. She offered to stay in a hotel, but I was hoping Connie could stay in your casita. It will only be one night. Monday night."

Before Sofia could stop herself, the word, "No!" shot out of her mouth.

It would be right in the middle of Harris's ten days.

Silence hung between them. Her sweet Abuela Rosa asked so little of her, but it wasn't a good time. She couldn't ask Harris to move out and then come back. Well, she could, but she didn't want to.

She knew she was being selfish, but this thing between them was just starting to gain traction. Or maybe it wasn't. She had no idea what Harris wanted to talk to her about at lunch. Who knew, he might tell her he'd had enough, and he was moving out.

Then again, he might not.

Ugh.

She'd never been good at thinking on her feet.

What she needed was time to process this. Time to hear what he had to say.

"Abuela, I'm sorry. Things are very hectic right now. You caught me off guard. May I call you later, and we can talk about it?"

"Certainly, *mija*. I didn't mean to bother you at work. Call me tonight after you get home. And if it's not convenient, I'm sure Connie wouldn't mind staying in a hotel."

All the way home, guilt over Abuela mingled with Sofia's nerves about the situation with Harris. When her phone rang again as she pulled into the driveway, she nearly jumped out of her skin. She shoved the car into Park and looked to see who was calling. A picture of her cousin Jacinta lit up the screen.

Sofia groaned and silenced the call.

Jacinta was, no doubt, calling to find out why Sofia hadn't offered an immediate yes to Abuela's request. There was no way she was going to talk to her cousin now when she didn't know the answer.

It wasn't as if she could say the casita was occupied. Jacinta would demand to know who was staying there. What was Sofia supposed to say? She didn't want to lie.

So, the best thing to do was not to pick up.

Her family had a tenuous relationship with boundaries. Sofia knew saying *It was not a good time* wouldn't hack it. Before she called Jacinta back, she needed to have an iron-clad reason in place.

Then again, if Harris had his bags packed, the casita might be free.

Her answer was waiting for her beyond the backyard gate.

Chapter Eight

Harris stood by the casita's kitchen table, his hands resting on the edge of a wrought-iron chair, staring down at the two sandwiches he'd picked up from the ER Grocery in town. His stomach was a tight knot, but not from hunger.

She had made the rules, and she'd broken them.

He wasn't sure what to do with that, and they needed to figure it out.

He checked the clock again. It was almost noon. Sofia would be home any minute. He knew she wouldn't be able to stay long—her salon schedule was always packed—but they needed to talk. *Really talk.* He wasn't mad about the kiss, not by a long shot. But he was confused, and more than anything, he needed to know where she stood.

Where *they* stood.

He heard the light knock on the front door of the casita.

"Come in," he called.

The door creaked open, and Sofia stepped inside.

"Hello," she said softly, closing the door behind her. She gave him a tentative smile, the kind that made his heart skip a beat.

"Hey." He smiled back, trying to keep his tone light, but the air between them was thick with unspoken tension.

"You mowed the lawn," she murmured. "Harris, thank you."

That was all it took to break the tension.

She looked gorgeous in jeans and the black blouse she was wearing; her sleek, shiny, dark hair salon-perfect. Beautiful, as always. Yet, despite her pulled-together appearance, he sensed that she was feeling slightly frazzled.

"I did. This morning."

"You don't know how much I appreciate it," she said. "Wish I could've been here to see it."

She lifted her brows, and they laughed.

"I know you don't have much time, so I picked up a couple of sandwiches for us," Harris said, gesturing toward the food. "I know you're busy, so I appreciate you taking your lunch here."

Sofia nodded. "Thanks. It's been...a morning."

He could see the nervous energy in her movements as she sat down at the table he'd set for them. He took a seat across from her and motioned to her plate. For a moment, they ate in silence. She kept glancing at him, then away, as if she was waiting for him to say something.

Finally, he set his sandwich down, cleared his throat, and leaned forward. "Sofia...about last night..."

Her eyes flicked up to his, a flash of hesitation crossing her face. She quickly swallowed the bite of food she'd been chewing, setting her sandwich down, too.

"Right. The kiss."

"Yeah, the kiss." Harris leaned back in his chair, giving her space but keeping his gaze steady. "You told me no kissing, no touching. I respected that because I didn't want to push you into anything you weren't ready for. But *you* kissed me."

Sofia bit her bottom lip, her fingers playing nervously with the edge of her napkin. "I know," she whispered, her voice barely audible.

Harris waited for her to continue, giving her time to collect her thoughts. When she didn't speak right away, he asked gently, "Why did you kiss me?"

She opened her mouth as if to say something, then shut it again. A flicker of vulnerability passed over her face. She looked down at the table, the silence between them stretching out. He could feel her hesitation, and part of him wanted to tell her it was okay, that they didn't need to talk about it. But the other part—the part that had been thinking about her nonstop since that kiss—needed an answer.

Finally, she sighed and met his eyes again. "I didn't plan to kiss you, but I… I couldn't help it. I'm attracted to you, Harris." Her voice was soft but honest, and Harris could hear the uncertainty in her tone. "Maybe we should use these ten days to…explore whatever this is between us."

Harris's chest tightened at her words, hope surging. "So, you're saying you want to give us a chance?" His voice sounded more eager than he intended, but he couldn't help it.

She nodded, still looking uncertain. "Maybe. I just don't want to make any promises I can't keep. This whole thing—us being married, accidentally or not—it's complicated. But I can't pretend I don't feel something for you."

Relief washed over Harris, but he kept it in check. "I agree. We should see where this goes. I've been thinking the same thing for a while now."

Sofia's lips twitched into a small smile, her shoulders relaxing slightly. "It's hard to believe how we got here. One night in Vegas and now…this."

Harris chuckled softly, the absurdity of their situation hitting him again. "Yeah, definitely not the way I imagined getting married."

Her smile grew a little wider, but then she looked down, her fingers tracing a pattern on the table. "This attraction between us…it's part of the reason we're in this mess in the first place."

He nodded, understanding what she was getting at. "I know. But since we both feel it, why are we fighting it?"

Sofia met his eyes again. The vulnerability was back. "I was afraid you might leave, Harris. After I kissed you, I spent the whole night thinking maybe I'd pushed you too far. I've been worried that all the chaos of my life—the kids, work, the rules that keep changing—would make you run. I don't want you to feel trapped."

Harris's heart squeezed at her words. He reached across the table and took her hand. "I would never just walk out on you, Sofia. And for the record, I like the chaos."

She let out a soft laugh, but her eyes remained serious. "It's just… I've been so hung up on what people would think. About me divorcing Dan, about maybe starting something new too soon. I mean, my marriage was over long before we officially ended it, but…"

Harris nodded. "I understand that. You were living apart for a while before you even filed."

"Yeah," Sofia said softly. "We were. But still, I've been scared of what people might say. But maybe it's time I stop worrying about that and just…let myself be happy."

Harris stood, pulling her up from her chair and into his arms. "I think we owe it to ourselves to see where this goes. To be happy."

Before she could respond, he bent down and kissed her deeply, his hands holding her close. Her arms slid around his neck, and for a moment, the rest of the world disappeared. All he knew was that it was even better than last night. This time, it felt like all the weirdness was gone. All that was left was the heat between them, the feel of her lips against his, and the undeniable connection that had been there from the start.

When they finally pulled apart, Sofia rested her forehead against his chest.

"That was exactly what I needed," she murmured, her voice slightly breathless. "We just can't do that in front of the kids. That's one rule that won't change."

He chuckled softly, brushing a strand of hair from her face. "I think I can live with that."

She answered by leaning in and planting a sweet kiss on his bottom lip. "Good, because I have to get back to work. I have a client coming in."

"I'll walk you out." He grabbed his keys and laced his fingers through hers as they walked toward the door. "Good news. The deck is an easy fix. All I need to do is pick up some things from the hardware store, and I should have it done by the time you and the kids get home."

"Save your receipts," Sofia said as he pulled the door shut. "I'll reimburse you."

He waved away her words. "It's the least I can do." Then he pulled her to him again and kissed her slowly, savoring the moment.

Her lips were soft and warm, and there was a new urgency in the way she clung to him. It wasn't like the kiss last night—hesitant and cautious...forbidden. This was the real deal, and for a moment, everything else disappeared. His heart thudded in his chest as he held her close, her body melting into his. As he deepened the kiss, he became vaguely aware of the fact that they were standing in her backyard, though the privacy fence would keep nosey neighbors from seeing them.

Because she didn't seem worried about it, neither was he. It was just the two of them in this moment.

No distractions.

No worries.

No hesitation.

When they finally broke apart, Sofia gazed up at him. "I'm glad I broke the rules," she confessed, her voice low and soft. "All my life, I've been such a rule follower."

"Yeah?" He chuckled. "That's kind of sexy."

"Yeah?" she asked, her dark eyes glistening.

The tension that had been building between them since the morning they'd woken up married was gone. Now, all that was left was a slow-burning flame that promised something more…much more.

If it didn't consume them first.

Harris wanted to pick her up and take her back inside and show her exactly how sexy he found her, but he knew she needed to get back to work. Instead, he found her lips again, claiming one last kiss. Greedily testing the theory, lost in this all-consuming need for her…

Until a voice from behind them shattered the stillness.

"*Oh!* Oh my gosh!" The voice was familiar.

They jumped apart like guilty teenagers.

Harris turned to see Jacinta Fortune, his cousin Micah's wife, standing just inside the gate, her eyes wide, her mouth agape.

There was no other way to say it. Their secret was out.

Sofia blinked and put more space between herself and Harris.

"Jacinta! I didn't hear you come in. What are you doing here?"

Jacinta's eyes darted between Sofia and Harris, as though she had caught them doing something illicit.

"I didn't know you two were…seeing each other," her cousin said, her brows arched.

Sofia reminded herself that she and Harris were married.

They weren't doing anything wrong. Still, Jacinta's accusatory tone made her feel like a teenager caught skipping school.

Sofia stepped forward, signaling to Harris that she would handle the situation. Instead of answering Jacinta, she said, "Harris, I know you have errands to run, and I need to talk to my cousin before I get back to the salon because I have a client in—" She glanced at her smartwatch. "In thirty minutes."

"You sure?" he asked.

Sofia nodded, praying he wouldn't try to kiss her, but also hoping, somehow, that he would. When he did, it was a relief. The kiss wasn't as intense as the one before Jacinta had interrupted, but it was more than a simple peck on the lips. It was a *statement*. It seemed to say that he wasn't upset their secret was out—and that realization fortified Sofia more than she expected.

"I'll see you tonight," Harris said, letting his hand linger on her shoulder. "I'll pick up something for dinner."

As he walked toward the gate, he glanced back at Sofia with a small, amused smile. The gate clicked shut, and she turned to face her cousin.

Jacinta gaped at her.

"Why are you looking at me like that?" Sofia demanded, crossing her arms.

"I'm not looking at you *like that*," Jacinta said, mimicking her stance. "This is just how my face is." She had one brow arched higher than the other, her lips pursed in a mix of surprise and judgment. It was a look Sofia knew all too well.

"What's going on, Sofia?" Jacinta crossed her arms over her chest, too, clearly waiting for an explanation.

"What do you mean?" Sofia asked, careful not to let Jacinta dictate the direction of the conversation—whether it would be about Abuela or Harris.

"You know exactly what I mean. I just caught you and Harris making out in the backyard."

"We weren't making out," Sofia said, though the heat rising in her cheeks suggested otherwise.

"Don't gaslight me. I know what I saw."

Sofia rolled her eyes. "It's none of your business."

"You were kissing my husband's cousin. I think that does make it my business."

Sofia clicked her tongue in annoyance. "Harris is a grown man. How does marrying his cousin entitle you to any insight into his love life?"

Jacinta pursed her lips in a way that made Sofia realize she had just dropped a significant chunk of information. Had she done that subconsciously? She wasn't sure.

A smile turned up the corners of Jacinta's mouth. "*Love life*, huh?"

Sofia's face flamed as she rubbed her arms nervously. "Look, it's…complicated."

"It didn't look very complicated to me," Jacinta quipped.

After a long, awkward pause, her cousin blew out a breath and softened her tone. "Look, you don't have to pretend around me. I've been your biggest advocate when it comes to getting back into dating after your divorce. Just be careful. Harris is family now. If things don't work out between the two of you, you'll still have to see him at family gatherings. So don't hurt him, okay?"

If Jacinta only knew the full story… Sofia made an exasperated sound. "I don't intend to hurt him. Again, this is none of your business."

"Fine," Jacinta conceded, though her eyes still sparkled with a greedy curiosity. "That's not why I came over anyway. Why won't you let Connie stay in the casita? You've upset Abuela. She's an old woman, Sofia. Don't be mean to her."

Sofia flinched.

"How is telling her I'd talk to her later being mean?"

It was hard to hear the criticism because Sofia adored Abuela. But she couldn't tell Jacinta the truth—not all of it…not the part about the marriage. So, she'd just have to deliver a partial truth.

"Harris is staying in the casita. He's fixing the deck and building a tree house for Jackson and a balance beam for Kaitlyn."

Jacinta eyed her skeptically. "He lives five miles away. Why does he have to stay here? He can't commute?"

Sofia bit her lip. She couldn't exactly tell her cousin that she and Harris had drunkenly gotten hitched in Las Vegas and were now trying to figure out if they wanted to stay married or go their separate ways. But then there were those kisses… And what they had agreed to a little while ago—things were changing fast.

"Jacinta," Sofia said, choosing her words carefully, "if you must know—and, as I've already said multiple times, it's really none of your business—Harris and I are trying things out, relationship-wise. Please respect that I don't owe you any more of an explanation than that. So, if you could help me out and keep this between us…the three of us…that would be great."

Jacinta's lips curved into a Cheshire cat grin. "I'll make a deal with you. Let Connie stay in the casita, and I'll keep my lips zipped."

Sofia's patience was wearing thin. "Since this is so important to you, why can't Connie stay at *your* house? I don't remember anyone else helping to pay for the casita. So I don't understand why the family feels entitled to treat it as their personal guesthouse."

"Well, if that's the way it has to be, I'll gladly welcome

Connie for the night. Abuela is important to me—and she should be to you, too," Jacinta said, conveniently glossing over the entitlement part of the conversation. "But go ahead and keep on playing tiny house with your boyfriend, who lives five miles away."

Sofia's temper flared. "Don't even go there. You know I love Abuela. She is extremely important to me, but I think our family needs to respect that this is my house. If I say no, I don't owe you an explanation."

Jacinta leveled her with a glare.

Sofia sighed, trying to rein in her frustration. "Look, there are reasons I can't and won't go into, but Harris has to keep staying in the casita. Jackson and Kaitlyn have been through a lot since the divorce, and I'm still being cautious. We've told the kids we're just friends, and that's how it has to be."

Jacinta pursed her lips. "That's an even better reason he should stay in the guest room." She paused, her eyes narrowing as she added, "Wait a minute, next week is their fall break, right? Aren't they spending the week with Dan?"

Sofia's heart sank. "That's right. Why?"

Jacinta slapped her hands together triumphantly. "The kids are gone. Harris can move into your house. Connie moves into the casita. Problem solved. You can thank me later."

Sofia stared at her cousin, speechless. How had this conversation spiraled so far out of her control? The truth was, everything had changed after her and Harris's conversation at lunch. Maybe they would give their relationship a real shot. But that didn't mean she was ready to uproot her life—or invite Connie to stay in the casita. Not yet.

She crossed her arms over her chest, her jaw tightening as she met Jacinta's smug gaze. "I'll think about it and let Abuela know when I call her tonight as promised."

Jacinta smiled as if she had won some sort of battle. For

now, Sofia would let her think she had and the situation was resolved.

But deep down, Sofia knew that nothing about this situation was settled.

Not even close.

Chapter Nine

Harris leaned back into the soft cushions of the sofa, relishing the warmth of Sofia's body against his. The room was dimly lit, the flickering light from the fireplace casting gentle shadows across her face.

Her presence, so close and intimate, felt natural. The quiet was only interrupted by the faint creaks of the house settling and the quiet hum of the refrigerator. A quiet peace, the likes of which Harris hadn't felt in a long time, settled over him.

Sofia's soft voice broke the comfortable silence. "I'm taking the kids to the Emerald Ridge Fall Festival this Saturday. I was wondering if you'd like to come with us?" She turned to him, her eyes searching his face. "If you want to experience family life, this will give you a good taste of it."

Harris grinned. "I can't even tell you how long it's been since I've gone to the fall festival. I went a couple of times as a kid. I remember how much I loved it."

"If you loved it so much, why haven't you been in so long?"

He shrugged, vague memories of carefree childhood days coming back to him. "Over the past decade, I've mostly been out of town when it happens. But I'd love to go with you."

Pausing, a thought crept into his mind. "But you know what that means, right? People will see us together, and they're bound to ask questions. Are you ready for that?"

Sofia took a deep breath and looked away for a moment as

if weighing the consequences. When she turned back to him, she shrugged. "Well, given the fact that Jacinta can't keep a secret, it's bound to get out sometime. At least this way, we can let the cat out of the bag on our terms." She smiled faintly. "Besides, it's not as if walking around the fall festival together means we're engaged. Or even serious, for that matter."

Her words, though said casually, tugged at Harris's heart. She was right. They were just testing the waters, but the more they were together, he found himself thinking about *more*— about the possibility of them as something real, something lasting. He was being careful not to rush her, even though the thought of a future with Sofia lingered in his mind like a tantalizing dream from which he didn't want to wake.

But what if he did wake up only to realize this bubble they were living in had burst and they couldn't make it work in the real world?

That scared the hell out of him.

"Speaking of Jacinta," he said, trying to shift the conversation to ease the weight in his chest, "how did things go with your cousin after I left?"

"Not bad," Sofia said, her voice lighter now. "Of course, Jacinta was surprised to see us together, but by the time I left to go back to work, she was all for us…" She shrugged, smiling. "Now that she's happily married to your cousin Micah, suddenly, it's her life's mission that I should find wedded bliss, too. Even though I've only been divorced for three months."

Harris raised an eyebrow, letting her words sink in.

Wedded bliss.

Could it really be possible for them? He wasn't sure, but he knew he was willing to explore whatever this was between them.

"Is that what you want?" he asked softly.

Sofia laughed, a small, nervous laugh that made him smile. "Let's not get ahead of ourselves," she said, her tone teasing.

He chuckled, but there was a part of him that couldn't stop wondering what it would be like to be married to her, to build a life together—one that wasn't rooted in what she called a drunken Las Vegas mistake, but in something *real*.

"Sounds like it could've gone worse," Harris mused. "But maybe next time, we should be a little more careful where we kiss."

Sofia's eyes twinkled. "Maybe. But I hope there won't be more surprises to complicate things. At least not like that."

He pulled her closer, resting his chin on the top of her head. "I think I can handle a few more surprises as long as they're with you."

Harris brushed his lips across her head, his heart feeling lighter in that moment. But before he could revel in the warmth of the night and the comfort of her presence, Sofia stirred slightly and spoke again, her tone a bit more serious this time.

"I'm glad you brought up Jacinta," she said. "I need to tell you something because, of course, nothing can be easy."

Harris frowned, his mind instantly alert. "What's going on?"

Sofia shifted so she could look at him directly, her expression conflicted. "Right before I left the salon to meet you for lunch today, I got a call from my abuela Rosa. It seems her best friend, Connie, is able to make a spur-of-the-moment visit. She'll be in town on Monday."

Harris nodded slowly, waiting for the rest of the story.

"Abuela asked if Connie could stay in the casita," Sofia continued, her voice tightening. "She caught me so off guard that I didn't know what to say."

"*This* Monday?" Harris asked, already feeling tension creep into his muscles. "Do you want me to leave?"

"No." Sofia snuggled in closer, her hand resting on his chest. "I don't want you to go."

Harris was torn. On the one hand, he should offer to vacate the casita for Connie. It was only fair. But on the other hand, things between him and Sofia were just starting to progress, and being close to her—and the kids—made everything easier. If he moved out, it might change the dynamic.

"What did you tell her?" he asked, still thinking through the logistics.

"I didn't give her a definitive answer," Sofia admitted, her brows furrowing slightly. "I just said it wasn't a good time to host a guest. She assured me Connie wouldn't be any trouble, that she just needed a place to sleep since Abuela's apartment is too small. I told her I was busy and I'd get back with her later."

Harris smiled sympathetically. "Does your family have the same problem with boundaries that mine does?"

Sofia rolled her eyes. "You have no idea. Case in point, Jacinta showing up unannounced."

"How did you leave things with her?" Harris asked.

Sofia sighed again. "She reminded me that the kids are going to Dan's house on Sunday for fall break. She suggested you move into the guest room in the house. Then Connie could stay in the casita. It would solve everything. But I don't know how you feel about that."

Harris blinked. He hadn't considered moving into the main house. He thought back to his earlier conversations with Sofia. The casita had been his buffer, a way to be close to her without crossing the lines she'd drawn. When the kids were at home, it wasn't an option. But with the kids going to their dad's, things were shifting. Was moving into the guest room in the house the next logical step?

She bit her lip and looked at him, her eyes uncertain. "I hate to ask you to move out because we agreed that you would have ten days in the casita. I feel like I'm changing the rules again."

Harris stared at her for a moment, his heart thudding in his chest. She wasn't pushing him away; if anything, she was bringing him closer. His mind raced with thoughts of what it would be like to be in the same house as Sofia, even for just a few days. To wake up and see her in the morning, to share the little moments of the day... It was tempting. *Too tempting.*

"What do you think?" Sofia asked, her voice soft but her gaze steady.

His thoughts whirled as he considered the possibilities, but one thing was certain: this was more than just about proximity. It was about trust and taking another step forward—together.

"I'd like that very much."

After Harris went back to the casita, Sofia sat at the kitchen table, her phone resting in her palm as she gathered her thoughts.

She'd promised Abuela she'd call her back tonight. After everything that had happened with Jacinta barging in and catching her with Harris, it was clear that she needed to speak to her grandmother. The sooner, the better.

She tapped Abuela's name in her contacts and took a deep breath as the call connected.

"*¡Hola, mija!*" Abuela's warm voice greeted her. "How are my babies today?"

"*Hola*, Abuela," Sofia said, her heart softening at the sound of her grandmother's voice. "The kids are doing well, busy as always. Kaitlyn's been practicing her cartwheels nonstop, and Jackson is counting the days until he sees his father."

"I can't wait to see them at the fall festival tomorrow," Abuela replied with a chuckle. "They're growing so fast. But tell me, what's going on with you, *mi amada nieta*?"

Sofia took a deep breath and dove in.

"Actually, Abuela, I wanted to say I'm sorry if I sounded abrupt when you called this morning. It was a busy morning, and you caught me at a bad time."

"Oh, *mija*, I should be the one apologizing to you. I should not have sprung that on you at work. I had just gotten off the phone with Connie and I was so excited about her visit that I wasn't thinking clearly."

"Abuela, no apology necessary. You're so important to me. I never want you to feel shoved aside. It was just one of those days. Will you forgive me?"

"You are very sweet to say that, Sofia. Let's agree that our apologies cancel the other out. Let it be water under the bridge. How was the rest of your day? I trust it was better?"

There was a note to Abuela's voice that made Sofia's stomach flip as her thoughts tipped back to Harris, their conversation in the casita and Jacinta's surprise visit.

"The rest of my day was much better than the way it started. It gave me time to think, and I realized I shouldn't have said no when you asked if Connie could stay in the casita. Of course, she's welcome. She can stay as long as she'd like."

There was a pause on the other end. "Are you sure, *mija*? If it's too much trouble, she can always stay at a hotel. Jacinta mentioned that you have a guest staying in the casita?"

Of course, she did. Jacinta can't keep her big mouth shut.

Her cousin's need to spill the beans was far greater than her ability to keep a secret. Had she really thought Jacinta *wouldn't* run straight back to Abuela and tell her that Harris was staying in the casita?

Now, it was a matter of how much her cousin had actually shared. Just the intel about Harris staying in the casita…which would raise plenty of questions on its own? Or had she also divulged that she'd caught the two of them mid-kiss? Sofia let the possibilities roll around in her head, bumping and crashing into each other like twin pinballs.

Finally, she realized she was relieved that at least part of her and Harris's secret was out in the open, but she would stick to her original plan and let Abuela be the one to bring it up.

"It's no trouble for Connie to stay in the casita, Abuela," Sofia said, doing her best to sound light and welcoming. "I'd love to have her stay with me. She's your best friend, and it's important to me that she feels welcome."

"Oh, eres tan bueno conmigo."

You are so good to me.

Sofia smiled at her abuela's words. She wanted to ask Abuela to tell Jacinta she'd said that since her cousin thought Sofia was mean and selfish, but the words dissolved on her tongue like sugar.

"But what will you do with your guest?"

Sofia slammed the door on the thought of what she'd like to do with Harris. This was her dear, sweet abuela. Sofia hoped the older woman couldn't read her mind.

"No worries," Sofia said. "The casita is free on Monday, and Connie is absolutely welcome."

"You are sure, *mija*?"

"I'm sure," Sofia insisted.

"Bueno, if you're sure," Abuela finally relented. "I'll tell Connie. She will be thrilled to stay at your place. It's been so long since she's visited. She will not be any trouble for you.

I promise. The two of us will be together the entire time that we are not sleeping. Then she will leave early Tuesday morning. You won't even know she's there."

"I will make sure the place is ready for her." Sofia was about to say good-night when Abuela made a humming noise that signaled she wasn't quite ready to hang up.

A pause followed, and her stomach twisted as she sensed what was coming next.

"What's this I hear about you and Harris Fortune? You're dating, *hmm*?"

Okay, here we go.

Sofia forced a smile, hoping that it would not allow the flicker of irritation at Jacinta's meddling that had resurfaced to show through in her voice. Again, she silently cursed her cousin's inability to keep a secret, but it dawned on her that Abuela hadn't asked why Harris had been staying in the casita. She'd only mentioned that she had *a guest*.

Maybe Jacinta had used some discretion?

"Well, Abuela…" Sofia chose her words carefully. "Harris and I have been spending time together. I guess you could say we're seeing where things go."

"I see," Abuela said, her tone pleased. "This sounds like good news, no? He's a good man, Sofia. Like his cousin Micah."

Yes, he was a good man.

Really, it was for the best that Jacinta and Abuela knew about Harris. They were taking the kids to the fall festival together tomorrow, and with that, the whole town would know. It was better to ease into it like this rather than try to explain why she'd hidden things.

Sofia smiled softly. "We shall see what happens, but I need to run and fix the kids' lunches for tomorrow."

They said good-night, and after she hung up the phone, Sofia exhaled, feeling a mix of relief and nerves.

Well, one secret was out.

She would have to guard the other one zealously—that they were married—because if word got out… She couldn't fathom the avalanche of repercussions that would unleash.

Chapter Ten

The fall festival was in full swing when Harris and Sofia arrived with the kids. The crisp October air carried the scent of barbecue smoke and caramel corn and the sound of a country band playing popular covers.

Sofia held Kaitlin's hand while Jackson walked beside Harris. The kids clutched small, pumpkin-shaped balloons that someone dressed in a scarecrow costume had given them as they'd approached the festival. Harris walked next to Sofia, close enough to feel the occasional brush of her arm against his.

Emerald Ridge Boulevard was closed off to cars. Vibrant fall decorations—pumpkins, hay bales and orange-and-red leaves—created a warm, festive atmosphere.

It appeared that the entire town had turned out for the annual event, which stretched through the heart of downtown. Booths lined both sides of the street, showcasing everything from handcrafted jewelry to farm-fresh goat cheese and baked bread to arts and crafts. There were apples and spices, and the festive hum of people talking, laughing and kids playing.

Jackson bounced along, talking about how he wanted to eat five caramel apples for dinner, while Kaitlin tugged at Sofia's arm, chattering excitedly about the pumpkin-carving contest.

Harris's memory of the festival was vague, but he knew it had never felt quite like this.

He glanced at Sofia and smiled. For the first time in a long time, he recognized the stirrings of something that almost felt…right.

He sucked in a deep breath prepared to confront the default setting in him that urged him to run like hell when he got too close to a woman, but tonight, it hadn't detonated.

Not yet, anyway.

"Mommy, look, horses!" Kaitlin cried, pointing to the long queue waiting for pony rides sponsored by the Walsh Equestrian Estate. "Can I ride?"

"The line is so long, *mija*," Sofia said. "Why don't we come back later and see if the wait isn't quite so bad? Surely, you don't want to spend your whole festival waiting to ride a horse."

The girl's face fell.

"I have an idea," Harris said. "Mr. Walsh, the owner of Walsh Equestrian, happens to be a good friend of mine. I'll bet I could set you and your brother up with some horseback riding lessons after you get back from your father's house. That way, you'd get to ride a horse for a lot longer than you'd get to ride here, and you won't have to miss out on the other fall festival fun because you're standing in line. How does that sound?"

The girl jumped up and down. "That sounds great!"

Sofia smiled at him and mouthed, *Thank you*. She blew him a kiss. Before Harris could react, Jackson exclaimed, "Mr. Harris! Look at all those hats!"

Harris chuckled as Jackson pointed to a display of Stetsons at a nearby vendor. "Let's go take a look," Harris said. "A guy can never have too many hats."

Sofia rolled her eyes playfully. "You probably have as many hats as I have shoes."

"Here's to ever-growing collections," Harris said.

"While you two look there, I'm going to help Kaitlin sign up for the pumpkin-carving contest," she said. "We'll meet you over there at Abuela Rosa's booth."

As Sofia walked toward the information booth, Harris led Jackson over to the hats. He picked up a deep brown Stetson with a wide brim and subtle, intricate leather detailing along the band. He placed it on the boy's head. Then he picked up another one, placed it on his own head and tipped it toward the boy.

"What do you think?"

The boy nodded enthusiastically.

Harris plucked the hat off of Jackson's head and held it up to the booth attendant. "Do you have hats in kids' sizes?"

The vendor nodded and pulled out a selection from under the wrap stand.

"Which one do you like?" Harris asked.

Jackson pointed to one similar to the adult-sized hat he'd been wearing a moment ago.

Harris put the hat on the boy's head, taking care to make sure it fit as it should.

"What do you think, bud?" he asked.

The boy studied himself in the mirror and said, "Yeah! I look like a cowboy."

"You sure do." Harris pulled out his wallet. "You're the real deal."

He said to the vendor, "We'll take it."

They met up with Sofia and Kaitlin at Abuela Rosa Chocolates booth, which was packed with customers admiring fall-themed creations—chocolate pumpkins, leaves, and even little chocolate hearts dusted with gold.

"What is this?" Sofia asked, tapping the brim of Jackson's hat.

"It's my hat, Mommy. Mr. Harris thinks I look like a real cowboy."

"That is an expensive hat, Harris." Her dark eyes were wide with concern.

"Every guy needs a good Stetson," he said.

Before Sofia could say anything, Jacinta spotted them and waved enthusiastically.

"Sofia! Harris!" she called, stepping out from behind the counter. Making her way through the crowd, she pulled her cousin into a quick hug. She glanced between Harris and Sofia with a knowing smile. "So…how's it going with you two?"

Harris felt the heat rise up his neck as he fumbled for a response, but Sofia just smiled, tucking a lock of hair behind her ear. "It's going well," she said simply. "How are things going with you, Jacinta?"

The woman's giddy smile was almost too big for her face. "Great. Just great. I'm very happy to see the two of you here. Together."

Sofia chuckled nervously, and Harris gave Jacinta a polite smile, grateful when she got pulled away by a customer asking about the chocolate truffles. As they continued walking, Sofia leaned into Harris, her hand slipping into his.

"That wasn't awkward at all," she whispered to Harris. "Sorry about that. I'm pretty sure the whole family knows now. Let me apologize in advance for anything they might say or do in regard to us being here together tonight."

It dawned on Harris that if Jacinta had told Micah, then his family probably knew he and Sofia were…uh…involved.

Harris squeezed her hand, a warmth spreading through his chest. "It's okay. Honestly, it's nice. Being out with you like this." His voice dropped slightly. "It feels good."

They walked farther down the street, weaving through the

crowd until they came upon The Style Lounge booth, where some of Sofia's team was busy putting colorful thread in people's hair. According to the sign, these were hair wraps, and they were also offering nail appliqués with tiny pumpkins and leaves.

"Sofia!" one of the stylists called, waving her over.

Kaitlin ran ahead and plopped down in the woman's empty chair.

"Heather, can you do a hair wrap for me?" the girl asked.

"You bet, darlin'," Heather said. "I can put pumpkins on your nails, too. If it's okay with your mom."

"Mommy, please?" Kaitlin pleaded.

"Sure," Sofia said. "Thank you, Heather."

The stylist nodded and began wrapping strands of thick thread around a thin section of Kaitlin's hair. As she worked, Heather looked back and forth between Harris and Sofia.

"*Girl!* What's going on here? I think you have some explaining to do."

The other stylists were busy, but they seemed to be leaning toward Sofia and Heather, no doubt listening.

Sofia sent Heather a pointed look, nodding discretely toward the kids, before giving a quick shake of her head.

Heather grimaced and then put her forefinger over her lips. She mouthed the word, *Sorry.*

"This is my friend, Harris Fortune." Sofia introduced the team to Harris.

As Sofia chatted, he stood back, keeping one eye on Jackson, who had wandered over to survey the offering of candy apples at the next booth. Sofia was in her element, confident and glowing. It was amazing how she effortlessly shifted between her role as boss and just being herself.

A moment later, Abuela Rosa appeared out of the crowd, waving at them.

"*Hola*, Abuela," Harris said. "It's nice to see you."

"*Hola*, Harris, it's good to see you." She took his hand in both of hers. "Refresh my memory. Did we meet at Jacinta and Micah's wedding?"

"Unfortunately, I wasn't able to attend. I was away on business."

Abuela laughed. "Oh, you Fortunes. There are so many of you I can't keep track. Well, it's good to meet you now. I approve of you and my Sofia."

A sly smile lit up her grandmother's face.

Sofia quickly wrapped up the conversation with Heather and hugged her abuela.

"Hello, we were just at the Abuela Rosa Chocolates booth. I was afraid we'd missed you."

"Here I am." The woman smiled and gave them a knowing look. "How about if I take the *niños* to see the kids' section? That way, you two can go and enjoy yourselves for a while."

"Kaitlin is getting a hair wrap," Sofia said. "And here's Jackson and his new hat."

Sofia wrinkled her nose at Harris. She looked adorable.

"Abuela!" The boy hugged his grandmother. "Look at my cowboy hat! Harris got it for me."

"It's very nice, lovey."

"Abuela, are you sure you're up for this?"

"You bet I am."

"Thank you so much," Sofia said. "I have my cell phone on me. Please call me if you need anything."

"It is my pleasure, *mija*," she said, taking Jackson by the hand.

"Mind your abuela," Sofia called over her shoulder, but the crowd had already come between them.

Harris and Sofia exchanged a look and continued their stroll. They walked a little further, reaching the part of the festival where booths were set up for games. There was an apple pie eating contest, a pin-the-face-on-the-pumpkin, a kids pool with plastic ducks—each duck came with a specific prize—and a tub where kids were bobbing for apples.

"Are you kidding?" Sofia murmured. "Can you imagine how germy that water is? Maybe I should text Abuela and tell her not to—"

She glanced up at him. Their gazes locked, and she put her phone into her pocket.

"I'm sure they will be fine," she said quickly.

He took her hand, and they walked, the festival's excitement and the chatter of passersby washing over them. This was their first real outing as a couple and there was a certain electricity in the air. Harris felt the weight of people's gazes on them as they made their way down Emerald Ridge Boulevard.

They passed a woman he didn't know, but he heard her whisper, "Are Harris Fortune and Sofia Gomez Simon dating?"

But he didn't mind. It felt…right.

As they approached the apple cider booth, the intoxicating aroma of fall spice drew them in.

"Would you like some?" Harris offered.

"Yes, please. Hot apple cider is one of my favorite things in the world."

Harris handed over a few bills and grabbed two steaming mugs, handing one to Sofia. They stood together near a booth that was selling artisan-made sterling silver jewelry, sipping the hot cider, their arms brushing occasionally as they watched people stroll by, laughing and enjoying the festival.

"This is so much fun," Sofia said. "I'm glad we're here together."

"Me, too." Harris flashed her a grin. "And it sure brings back memories."

"I'm surprised I never ran into you here," she said. "Then again, I was usually working the booth and the crowd is so large, you could've been here. We might've been standing right next to each other and not even realized it."

"I would've realized it if I'd been standing next to you."

"Yeah?" she asked softly.

"Definitely."

Something smoldering passed between them.

Sofia smiled and seemed like she was at a loss for words. Her gaze fluttered down to the cup in her hands, and she lifted it to her lips and sipped her cider.

Then she turned and began sifting through a tray of earrings. She picked up the pair of delicate silver earrings shaped like leaves, simply elegant yet beautiful, just like her. She held them up and gazed at herself in the mirror that was on the jewelry case before returning them to the tray.

"Those are pretty," he said. "Would you like them?"

"Oh my gosh, no, thank you," Sofia said and walked away from the booth. "And speaking of expensive gifts. I can't believe you bought that hat for Jackson. Please tell me he didn't ask you to buy it."

"He didn't. I told him to pick one out. That was all on me."

"I wish you wouldn't have done that," she said.

Harris shrugged.

"Thank you," she added. "It was unnecessary but very much appreciated. You made a little boy very happy."

She stopped suddenly and turned to face him. "I just don't want you to get the wrong idea."

"What kind of wrong idea are you talking about?"

She sighed and looked him square in the eyes. He could see her mind working. "How do I say this?"

"Just say it," he said.

"When we were in Vegas, I remember you saying something about women who dated you for what they could get."

Harris's brows lifted.

"I'm not like that, Harris."

"I know you're not. You haven't asked me for a thing. You even turned down the diamond wedding band when we were—"

"Shhhh!" she hissed, looking around them, assessing who might've been close enough to hear.

He realized in that moment that he didn't really care who knew they were married. Would it steer her away from the annulment if someone found out?

But he wouldn't do that to her. He wouldn't force her hand. He wanted her to realize that she wanted this marriage as much as he did.

Because he did.

Did he?

He blinked at the thought. Digesting it. Giving the inner voice that always urged him to cut and run when a woman got too close a chance to warn him this wasn't right.

But it was not pushing him away.

If anything, it was suggesting that staying married to Sofia Gomez might be the right thing to do.

Might.

Maybe.

"Let's go sit down for a moment." He gestured toward an empty picnic table under a tree.

He held her hand while she lifted one boot-clad foot over the bench, sat down and settled in.

He sat next to her. They were so close, their knees were touching under the table.

"I was engaged to someone who, it turned out, was in it for the money," he confided. "I thought she was the one. But a few weeks before the wedding, she let it slip that she didn't want kids. She said if we had them, she'd want a surrogate and a nanny to deal with the *little monsters*."

He shook his head, the words still stinging after all this time. "She was more interested in my money and the Fortune name than in building a family. I called off the wedding. I guess, after that, I became a lot more guarded. It was harder to trust people."

Sofia gave his hand a gentle squeeze. "I'm sorry, Harris. That must've been hard."

"It was," he admitted, glancing at her. "I'm telling you this because that experience opened up some kind of internal radar. Believe me, I know when a woman is dating me for what she can get. You are *not* that kind of woman."

Sofia gazed at him. "No, I'm not. In fact, sometimes it's difficult for me to accept gifts from people. I'm really sorry that happened to you."

Harris shrugged.

"If anything good came out of it, I realized how important family is to me. Losing my parents as a kid altered my life forever."

Sofia inhaled an audible breath.

"After they died, I thought that the only way I'd get that sense of family back was if I built one of my own. Amanda, my ex-fiancée, didn't want that."

Sofia was quiet for a moment before speaking. "I can understand that. Family is everything to me, too."

"Harris Fortune," said a familiar female voice.

Harris glanced over his shoulder and saw his sisters, Priscilla and Zara, grinning as they approached. He groaned inwardly, already dreading the inevitable questions.

"Hey, big brother," Priscilla called out at him. "Looks like the rumors are true. Look at the two of you. You're so cute together."

"Oh, hey, you two," Harris said. "I think you know Sofia Gomez Simon. Sofia, these are my sisters, Zara and Priscilla."

"How did I *not* know you were dating?" Zara added, her smile mischievous.

"Well, that's because…" Harris looked at Sofia, trying to gauge how much he should divulge.

"We are enjoying each other's company," she said.

Simple and truthful.

Priscilla and Zara exchanged delighted glances. He shot them both a look, a silent warning not to push too far. That's when he noticed that Priscilla was wearing a money belt and carrying a sign that was now hanging down by her side, and Zara was holding a Polaroid camera.

"What do you have there?" Harris nodded to the sign.

Priscilla held it up. It said, Kiss Under the Falling Leaves and Help Raise Money for a Good Cause.

"What are you two up to?" Harris asked.

Priscilla glanced down at the sign. "We are raising funds for the Emerald Ridge Thanksgiving Fund. One hundred percent of all donations go to the Emerald Ridge Food Pantry to help provide traditional Thanksgiving dinners for those in need."

Harris reached for his wallet and pulled out five twenty-dollar bills. He handed them to Priscilla.

"Thanks," she said. "That's very generous, Harry."

Priscilla stepped toward them and held up a small bouquet of brightly colored fall leaves attached to a fishing pole.

"What's that?" Sofia asked.

A wicked grin spread over Zara's face. "For every donation, you get to kiss under the fall leaves. It's our take on kissing under the mistletoe—Fall edition." She held up her camera. "And you get a souvenir picture. Since you gave such a generous donation, Harry, I'll give you two pictures: One for each of you. Ready?"

Priscilla held out the fishing pole so the leaves dangled over Harris and Sofia's heads.

"You okay with this?" he whispered to Sofia.

"Anything for a good cause," she said, her face lighting up.

Harris pulled Sofia into his arms. He dipped his head and captured her lips in a tender, slow kiss. He heard the zip of Zara's camera as she captured the moment on film…twice.

In the background, the sound of hoots and cheers erupted around them, but Harris didn't care. When Sofia didn't pull away, everything else faded away.

That was all that mattered.

She was all that mattered.

The feel of her in his arms.

The warmth of her kiss.

For one timeless moment, they were the only two people in the world, except for the faraway sound of Zara saying, "Um, I guess I'll leave your pictures here. On the table."

When they finally pulled apart, both of them slightly breathless, his sisters were gone.

Sofia grinned. "Well, if it wasn't already, I guess our secret is out, *Harry.*"

Harris chuckled, leaning his forehead against hers. "I think it's safe to say the whole town knows now. And I'm okay with that."

Chapter Eleven

On Sunday evening, Sofia pulled into her driveway as dusk was putting the day to bed. She had delivered the kids to Dan in Waco, which was the halfway point between Emerald Ridge and Austin. The drive back alone had been mostly peaceful, with the radio humming low in the background, but her mind had been a riot.

Handing off the kids always upended her nerves. This time it was even more complicated now with Harris in the picture. She turned off the minivan's engine and stared at the soft, amber glow of the porch light.

Home at last.

Her sanctuary.

The kids would be with their father until Wednesday, when she met Dan in Waco again to collect them.

In the meantime, she and Harris would be alone. Just the two of them and the promise of him moving into the guest room when Connie arrived tomorrow night.

As she slid out of the van, Harris stepped out onto the porch, his broad frame silhouetted against the doorway. The sight of him standing there sent a strange flutter through her.

He smiled, and that warm, easy grin of his set loose a kaleidoscope of butterflies.

"Hey," he greeted her, stepping forward and wrapping her in a tight hug as soon as she reached him. "I missed you."

Sofia leaned into him, inhaling his familiar, sexy scent—sandalwood and leather. His arms were strong around her, grounding her. After the tense exchange with Dan, this was exactly what she needed.

After she and Harris stepped inside and closed the door on the world, she followed Harris into the kitchen, where he picked up a gorgeous bouquet of fall flowers—orange and yellow roses surrounded by rust dahlias and mums, with eucalyptus and other greenery.

"These are for you," he said.

She buried her nose in them. "That's so sweet, Harris. Thank you."

He handed her a glass of red wine. "How did the drop-off go?"

Sofia sighed and sipped the wine. It tasted like figs, blackberries and vanilla, with a hint of clove and a mustiness that suggested it was probably expensive. She let the smooth, velvety flavor coat her tongue before answering.

"It was…fine, I guess. I told Dan that you were staying in the casita for a few days because it was bound to come up when the kids mentioned you fixing the deck."

"And how did he take that?" Harris asked.

Not well.

Sofia shrugged. "He doesn't really have a choice in the matter."

After they'd settled the children in the back seat of Dan's car, he'd said, "I need to talk to Mommy for a minute."

He'd mansplained the dangers of having a strange guy hanging around, followed by a lecture about how important it was for *her* to set a good example for her children.

Then she'd showed him the photo of the blonde sitting on his lap that Jacinta had texted her, and asked if his girlfriend would be hanging around while the kids are with him.

Dan had gaped at the picture. "How did you get this?"

"It doesn't matter, Dan. I hope you'll apply the same rules while you have the kids. At least both of us know the Fortune family. I have no idea who this woman is."

Then he'd turned the tables and played the martyr, saying, "Mmm. So, you've snagged yourself a Fortune. I guess he can give you all the things I never could."

She'd wanted to say no amount of money could buy her what she wanted...what she *needed* in a relationship...but he hadn't understood that before the divorce. Why would he understand now?

So, she'd simply told him she needed to go, gave another round of hugs, kisses and I-love-yous to the kids and headed back to Emerald Ridge.

The exchange with Dan had unfolded quietly, in civil tones. To the uninitiated, it might've seemed like a pleasant conversation.

That, in a nutshell, summed up why their marriage had failed. It was a pretty package hiding a whole lot of ugliness inside.

Harris was watching her, studying her as if he was trying to read between the lines.

She didn't want to talk about Dan and invite his specter to elbow its way between Harris and her tonight, but she felt like she owed it to him to say, "I'm not hung up on my ex-husband, Harris. I'm not in love with him. That ship capsized a long time ago. He's the father of my children. The kids were happy to see him and excited to spend some of their break with him. That's all that matters."

Harris nodded. The subject was settled. He gestured to the French doors. "Come out here. I have a surprise for you."

He had worked so hard the past couple of days. Yesterday, before they'd gone to the fall festival, he'd stained the deck.

He'd mentioned that it would need twenty-four hours to dry. She couldn't wait to see it.

The blinds that covered the doors were closed. Harris reached out and opened one of the doors a crack. The aroma of some kind of meat sizzling on the grill drifted in. Her stomach growled in appreciation.

"Are you grilling steaks?" she asked.

"I am. Come out here while I take them off the grill. They'll need to rest for a few minutes before we eat."

"A steak dinner is a fabulous surprise. Thank you." She rose on her tiptoes and planted a kiss on his lips. He looped his arm around her waist and pulled her close.

"I hope the grill wasn't in too bad a shape," she said. "It's been a long time since anyone fired it up."

Since long before Dan had moved to Austin.

He grimaced. "Yeah, it had seen better days. I picked up a new one."

"Oh, okay." Visions of a small, stainless steel portable grill flashed through her mind. He would be able to take it home with him when he left… The thought of him leaving whooshed through her, leaving a wake of sadness.

She blinked it away. They had more than a week before the end of their ten-day trial. She was not going to think of endings and spoil the evening.

"Close your eyes," Harris commanded softly. He was facing her, his back against the door, his hand perched behind him on the door handle.

"Why?" Sofia asked. "What are you up to?"

"To get the full effect of your surprise, you need to be out on the deck."

"What…?" She laughed.

"Just trust me."

Of course. He probably wanted her to see his handiwork

from the best angle. So, she went along with it, closing her eyes and letting him lead her outside.

When they were there, he said, "Okay, open your eyes."

She did, and her mouth fell open.

The refurbished deck looked gorgeous under the soft glow of the lights that Harris had strung up. How had he known she'd always wanted market lights? She looked at him, but the words lodged in her throat.

She looked back at the deck. The wood gleamed, freshly stained and smooth, a testament to Harris's hard work.

A grouping of wrought-iron furniture—tasteful and elegant—and a cozy, porch bed-swing hung off to the side under a brand-new pergola erected near a bronze fire pit. None of this had been there when she'd left for Waco this morning.

Neither had the table. It was beautifully set with her dishes atop a new tablecloth of warm autumn hues, along with a small vase of flowers similar to the ones Harris had handed her when she'd gotten home, and flickering candles that cast a soft, romantic glow graced the center of the table.

All she could do was gape at it.

It was like one of those television shows where the owner goes out for the day and a team of designers comes in and transforms the place.

"Harris...what did you do?" she gasped, finally finding her words. "How did you...?"

"Surprise," he said.

Sofia smiled, her heart swelling with affection for this generous man.

He was *too* generous.

"Harris, this is gorgeous, but it's too much. I appreciate the gesture, but the furniture...it's not in my budget. We'll have to return it."

Harris shook his head. "It's a gift, Sofia. You don't have to worry about the cost."

"No."

"Yes," he said. "Final sale. No returns."

She doubted that, but...

"You're spoiling me," she complained, setting down her wineglass on the table and crossing her arms, her voice gentle and a bit hesitant.

"Good. You deserve to be spoiled," he replied, gathering her into his arms, his lips hovering a breath away from hers, sending a thrill of want and need coursing through her. "It gives me pleasure to spoil you."

She opened her mouth to protest, to say something about not wanting to seem like she was in this for his money—but the look in his eyes stopped her. Plus, they'd already had that discussion at the fall festival.

"Thank you, Harris. This is exactly the patio furniture I would've picked out myself. How did you know?"

"I just knew," he said with a wink, and she couldn't help but laugh.

Dinner was delicious. Harris had gone all out, grilling a thick, juicy T-bone to perfection, alongside roasted asparagus, baked potatoes and a crisp garden salad. But more than the food, it was the quiet moments—catching each other's gazes across the table, the easy conversation—that made the night feel special.

They joked about being an old married couple. But tonight felt like their "real" first date. At the fall festival, the kids had been with them.

So, this really *was* the real first date.

Harris raised his glass to hers. "To new beginnings."

"Cheers," Sofia murmured, feeling a sexy warmth spread through her body. Not just from the wine, but from the way

Harris was looking at her, like she was the only person in the world.

They were alone…no kids in the house…no family barging in.

She hadn't felt this way in so long. She hadn't realized just how much she missed the simplicity of two people being together and enjoying each other's company. She felt seen and cherished for who she was, not for who the other person wanted her to be.

After dinner, Harris said, "I hope you saved room for dessert."

"I'm stuffed," she groaned, holding up her hands. "I can't eat another bite."

Harris chuckled. "Everyone has a separate dessert stomach. No matter how full you are, there's always room for dessert."

She raised an eyebrow, amused. "Is that so?"

"Yep. I got *tiramisu* for us."

Sofia groaned again.

He smiled and disappeared inside.

The evening's chilly air made the warmth of the fire pit and the bed-swing's cozy blankets even more inviting. Sofia took her wine and moved to the swing by the fire pit.

Watching Harris through the kitchen window, she sighed contentedly. She loved how at home Harris seemed to be in her kitchen…and around her…comfortable in his own skin.

They were good for each other.

Tonight, it seemed like they had always been together. Only this relationship wasn't limiting. They built each other up rather than tearing each other down.

Then again, no matter how familiar it felt, they'd only known each other a week and a day. They were still in the honeymoon stage of the relationship.

Harris returned with a bowl containing a large portion of tiramisu, grabbed his wine and settled beside Sofia. She snuggled into him as the swing gently swayed.

He scooped up a bite of the dessert and offered it to her.

Sofia relented, letting him feed it to her. The creamy sweetness melted on her tongue, and she sighed happily. "Oh my gosh, this is delicious. Maybe one more bite. Then the rest is yours."

Harris smiled and fed her another bite.

As the fire crackled and the evening air grew cooler, Sofia pulled the Sherpa fleece blanket over them and snuggled closer to him, resting her head against his chest. She could hear the steady rhythm of his heart, feel the warmth of his body, and for the first time in what felt like forever, she felt... safe.

And happy.

Despite the way reality would intermittently intrude, reminding her that this wasn't just a date. And Harris wasn't just a man she was getting to know—he was her husband. Accidentally, yes, but still... Soon enough, they would have to decide what they were going to do.

Could they actually make it work?

She didn't have to figure out everything tonight. She would live in the moment, enjoy the warmth of Harris's arms around her and the feeling of everything being right.

If only for right now.

"So the kids are gone until Wednesday, right?" Harris murmured.

"Yes."

"You know what we should do while they're away?" His voice sounded low and teasing.

Sofia smiled, her cheek still resting against his chest. "What should we do?"

"We should fly to Paris."

Sofia laughed. "Okay, here we go with Paris again. This seems to be a theme when we start drinking."

Harris shook his head. "I'm a little relaxed, sure, but I'm not drunk. I mean it. Do you want to go?"

She pulled back slightly, gazing up at him, her brow furrowed. "You know, someday I'm going to call your bluff. Someday, when you ask me if I want to go to Paris on a whim, I'm going to say yes."

Harris smiled and traced her jawline with his thumb. "Well, *someday* I hope you will call my bluff because that suggests we have a future together. However, there's no time like the present. Let's go."

Sofia shook her head, laughing softly. "Harris, I have to meet the kids on Wednesday. You know I can't just pick up and go. It's Sunday night. That would give us, what, two days at most?"

"But wouldn't it be romantic?" he pressed, his eyes sparkling with mischief. "Dinner in Paris, a night at the Ritz, maybe a stroll along the Seine, and a kiss in front of the real Eiffel Tower?"

She sighed, the idea tugging at her heart. "It sounds like a fairy tale. But the first time I see Paris, I want it to be more than a whirlwind trip. I want time to take it all in."

"I get that," he said, his voice soft. "But you can always return. Sometimes, you just have to say, 'I'm doing this.' You can't let the things that are holding you back get in the way. If you take a leap of faith, sometimes the obstacles end up working themselves out."

Sofia gazed at him for a long moment, her heart swelling with emotions she couldn't quite name.

What if she said yes? What if she said, *Let's do it*?

For a moment, she let herself go there. In her head, she

imagined she was a free spirit who could grab her toothbrush and go.

She couldn't do it. It wasn't who she was.

It didn't matter anyway because she wasn't entirely sure Harris was serious. What if it was some kind of a test to see if she was in this for him…or for his money?

But that was even more ridiculous. He was the one who had offered. She hadn't asked.

She gazed up at Harris, and he leaned in, closing the space between them. He kissed her softly, letting the subject of Paris drop…much to her relief.

"You know," she whispered, "Abuela's friend, Connie, won't be here until tomorrow afternoon. Tonight, we have this big, private backyard all to ourselves."

"You're not afraid that your cousin is going to come barging in?"

"She wouldn't dare."

Harris kissed her again. It was heady, intoxicating.

She concentrated on the moment, pushing away the shadows of her past and silencing the voices in her head that questioned the future. She was kidding herself if she thought she was the kind of woman who could just drop everything and jet off to Paris.

But tabling the conversation didn't seem to bother him.

Even if their lives didn't exactly align, right now, in this moment, their bodies promised to fit perfectly together.

Sofia surrendered and let herself be transported by his kiss, forgetting everything but the feel of his lips on hers and his hands on her body.

She melted into him, the cool night air forgotten, as his warm lips trailed down her throat. Every inch of his presence ignited a desire the likes of which she hadn't felt in a very long time.

It was a need she didn't know how to voice. Their one
night together in Las Vegas—their wedding night—was a
hazy memory, but tonight was vivid and real. She wanted to
make love to him right here in the open air, on the bed-swing
he'd so thoughtfully given her, underneath the stars.

Harris's mouth brushed the tender skin of her neck, sending shivers coursing through her body. Her breath caught in
her throat as he looked at her with hooded eyes and a sul-
try smile.

Until now, she hadn't let herself acknowledge how much
she had wanted this moment. She tucked her face into the
curve of his neck, inhaling that delicious scent of sandalwood
and leather. She breathed in deeply. It was so distinctly Harris, and it hit her hard.

Harris must've sensed the shift because he pulled back
slightly. "Are you okay? Is *this* okay?"

She was searching for the words, but everything that came
to mind seemed inadequate to let him know how absolutely
okay it was—that she wanted his hands on her, needed his
body inside her.

When she didn't immediately answer, he tilted her face up
to his. His thumb grazed her forehead, sweeping back a lock
of hair that had fallen into her eyes before his lips found the
newly exposed skin. The gentleness of that gesture, so intimate, so caring, made her heart skip a beat.

She nodded, and he searched her eyes. Her fingers raked
through his hair, pulling him closer as her lips parted, inviting him in, permitting him to take all of her. The kiss was
soft at first, then deeper, more impatient. Her fingers tangled
in his thick hair, pulling him closer as their kiss grew fever-
ish, all-consuming.

She wanted—needed—more of him…

He seemed to understand, because she barely registered

the moment her sweater disappeared or when his jeans fell away—until they were naked, lying together, skin against skin, under the warm blanket.

The way he took possession of her left her gasping.

He explored every inch of her. His touch was electric, igniting something primal inside her. One of his hands splayed over her breast, his fingers, work-callused from the handiwork he'd done, teasing her nipples and sending jolts of pleasure straight through her. His touch was gentle as his fingers danced down her belly. His touch made her muscles tighten with anticipation. Then, finally, his hand dipped lower, teasing, seeking, until his fingers found her center. Sofia gasped, her back arching as he stroked her, coaxing moan after moan from her lips.

Harris's hands found hers. Their fingers laced together. He hesitated for a brief moment as if offering her one last chance to stop, to pull away. But Sofia didn't want to stop. Her heart raced in anticipation. Her body thrummed with a red-hot need. She wanted him—*needed* him.

As if he sensed her silent plea, Harris was on top of her, and in one slow, fluid movement, they were one.

The first thrust stole her breath, her thoughts and any shred of sanity she had left. A soft moan escaped his lips as they found a rhythm together, each movement in sync, each glide taking her further from reality. His intensity was overwhelming, but Sofia welcomed it, her hands clutching his shoulders, her legs wrapped around his waist, pulling him deeper, closer.

Every thrust, every movement, was filled with a need that matched her own, their bodies demanding more, taking and giving until they both reached that breaking point. When they finally exploded together, Sofia was left breathless, her heart racing as if it might burst from her chest. She had never known such ecstasy, such pure pleasure.

Bodies spent and tangled, Harris lay atop her, still inside her, his presence so deep she swore he could touch her heart. The weight of him felt protective, like a shield from the outside world. Sofia held on to him, her fingers tracing lazy circles along his back as they both came down from the high.

He turned over onto his side, pulling her close to him. She could've stayed like that forever, wrapped in his warmth, his strength, his love.

Reality was beginning to come back into focus, but for now, she pushed all thoughts of the past and the future out of her mind. All that mattered was the present—the intoxicating heat of their shared desire.

In that moment, nothing else existed but Harris and her entwined together.

She felt safe.

Wanted.

Loved.

Chapter Twelve

The next morning, Sofia tried to ignore the flicker of uncertainty that gnawed at her insides, despite the otherwise perfect evening she and Harris had shared last night.

They'd ended up in her bed, where they'd spent the night together, making love twice more and snuggling until morning. The lovemaking was phenomenal. In fact, it was proving it could be downright addictive.

So, what was wrong with her? Why was she feeling so… *off* when she should be happy?

It was Monday morning, which meant she didn't have to work at the salon today. He'd greeted her with coffee and bagels in bed. He'd asked her to spend the day with him and said he had planned something special.

He was making a good case that he just might be the unicorn—the perfect man.

Maybe that was the problem? In her experience—at least with her first marriage—everything seemed perfect, then took an abrupt nosedive. She wasn't so delusional that she believed relationships always had to be flawless, that there would be no bumps in the road… But everything was happening so fast with Harris that she needed time to catch her breath, to sort it all out and put it in order.

She and Dan had been together since before she'd even understood the implications of married life…of family life.

Except for the brief time they had been separated and then divorced, she'd never been alone. She had to admit she hadn't hated the time on her own. It made her feel strong and capable, and yes, sometimes she was lonely, but that was okay.

She couldn't help but wonder if she was meant to be alone for a while, to spend some time by herself, getting to know herself, rather than jumping into another marriage so fast?

Then life had plunked Harris Fortune down in the big middle of everything.

Harris and his expensive gifts and wines and perfect body... All of that had a way of creating a noise in her head that made her heart ignore reality and take a swan dive into... Into *what*?

The chance of life with a partner who seemed to understand her and loved her kids...?

What was wrong with her? She needed to be grateful and gracious.

As Harris entered the room, she smiled at him and slipped into her jacket, hoping that he couldn't see through her to the ugly, acidic indecision eating up her insides.

"Are you ready for your next surprise?" he asked as they stepped out onto the front porch.

"All these surprises, Harris..." She tried to keep her voice light as she locked her front door. "You're definitely spoiling me."

"It's fun to spoil you. Trust me, you'll like this one."

He opened the passenger door of his midnight-blue Porsche, and she slid onto the plush beige-leather seat.

It was so easy to be with him—the playful gleam in his eyes, the way he made her feel so special. She wished she could let go and simply enjoy the moment, but the truth was she was *terrified*.

Terrified because she couldn't tell if he was being so good

to her because he was trying to win her over… You know, the old thrill of the chase.

Or was she overthinking everything?

Could he really be this wonderful and she was an idiot for not realizing it?

As they drove through the quiet streets of Emerald Ridge, there was a crackle in the air. It was probably just her, but there was a tension running through Sofia like an electrical current. If Harris pushed too hard, he might get shocked.

"Where are we going?" she asked.

"My house," he said.

Oh! Okay, that was a surprise. A nice surprise.

She wanted to see where he lived and learn more about him. She lifted her shoulders and let them drop, letting go of the tension.

Clearly, she needed to take a breath and go with the flow.

Before too long, they turned onto the long driveway of the Fortune compound. She knew this was the Fortunes' property. Everyone in Emerald Ridge knew that. Even so, the sight of the sprawling estate looming in the distance made her stomach flutter with peculiar unease.

It was…fancy. And nice. She hoped he wasn't going to surprise her by introducing her to his family. If that were the case, she would've spent more time on her hair and makeup. She would've chosen something different to wear.

And that was a red flag because she was who she was, and she did not put on airs. Not even for the Fortunes.

When he steered the car away from the grand estate, she let out a silent sigh of relief. They drove for a moment, passing several McMansions privately tucked away on the grounds.

"Who lives in those houses?" she asked.

"My siblings and I each have a house on the property," he said. "My uncle Sander lives in the main house."

She knew his brother, Roth, in passing, and had met his sisters, Zara and Priscilla, at the fall festival on Friday. They seemed like nice people. They were down-to-earth in a way that made it a jolt to realize that they lived in such grand homes. In her encounters with them, they'd seemed so...common. It was an old-fashioned word that Abuela Rosa often used—as a compliment—to describe someone who was relatable and didn't put on airs.

However, Sofia knew good and well that the Fortune family was anything but *common*.

Harris was no exception. His house was an imposing two-story brick structure with white columns. It looked like it belonged on the pages of *Southern Living* magazine. It was beautiful but intimidating in a way that suggested it might have stories that she couldn't relate to.

Harris stopped the car on the semicircular brick driveway. "Welcome to my humble abode," he said.

"*Humble*, huh?"

He smiled at her and unfolded his body from the car, walked around and opened the door for her.

As they approached the red-lacquered double front doors, she chewed on the fact that she'd always wanted a red front door, but Dan thought it was too much. Why hadn't she painted her front door after he'd moved out? She added the task to her mental to-do list as the meticulously manicured flower beds snagged her attention. Located on either side of the front porch, they were laden with marigolds, mums and snapdragons in gorgeous autumn colors. It was breathtaking.

She, too, could have beautiful flowers if she had a grounds-keeper to do it for her. Then, the reality that she should hire the teenager across the street to mow her grass before she coveted Harris's flowers elbowed aside the snarky thought.

As he unlocked the front door, she hesitated on the porch,

taking in the splendor. She'd known Harris lived well, but this? This was on another level. The scale of it, the sheer luxury, sent another wave of doubt coursing through her.

"Come on in," Harris said, offering his hand. His touch was warm and surprisingly grounding.

She stepped through the doors into the grand foyer, and her breath caught. High ceilings towered overhead, and a sweeping staircase curved elegantly toward the second floor. Off to the right, a formal living room looked picture-perfect, as if plucked straight from a catalog. She didn't have time to absorb the details because Harris was already moving down the hallway. The air smelled faintly of furniture polish, the kind of scent that hinted at a space kept pristine, maybe a little *too* pristine.

They stopped in a sleek kitchen, all crisp white and glass cabinets, gleaming stainless steel and marble countertops. It was impressive, sure, but also too perfect. She'd never be able to wipe her kids' fingerprints off of those stainless steel appliances.

"How about a cup of coffee?"

"That sounds great."

"Your house is lovely," she said, trying to sound casual. "It suits you—modern, but it has charm."

"Thanks," he said absently as he brewed the coffee in a pod machine.

"Do you spend much time here?" she asked.

"Until recently, not as much as I'd like. I know I told you I travel a lot and my primary residence is in Dallas.

"But I'm here for the foreseeable future. My siblings and I have some family business we're working through, and then there's the matter of Linc Banning's murder."

He'd confided that he and Linc used to be close, but— "Why is Linc's murder keeping you here?"

He handed her the coffee and shrugged, a sadness knitting his brow. "I don't know. I just feel as if I owe it to him."

"Owe what to him?" she asked.

He studied her for a moment before saying, "Linc and I were like brothers once. We lost touch after his mom, Delia, passed away a few years ago. I feel like I let him down. Why don't we take our coffee into the living room? I'll light a fire in the fireplace."

Sofia had so many questions, like how exactly he was planning to make things square with his dead friend. Hunt down Linc's killer himself? The thought made her shiver. If Harris started poking his nose into places it didn't belong, it could have far-reaching implications. No amount of Fortune money could keep him—or her kids, for that matter—safe from a murderer intent on not being caught.

The person had killed once, who knew if he or she had any compunctions about killing again to keep from being exposed. She was tempted to tell him that he needed to leave the sleuthing to the authorities, but the way he'd shut down the conversation made it clear he didn't want to talk about it anymore.

If she and Harris were going to build a future together, they'd have to revisit the conversation because it could be a matter of safety for her children.

They'd talk about it sometime, but not now.

She was getting ahead of herself.

As Sofia tried to put the thought of killers on the loose out of her mind, her gaze was drawn to the deep charcoal Chesterfield sofa in the living room. She hadn't noticed it when they'd first entered the house, but there it was with its velvet upholstery, plush rolled arms and brass nail trim.

It was her dream sofa—for after the kids were grown. It gave the room an air of classic elegance, while the cognac-colored leather armchair across the room from it offered a more masculine touch.

Clearly, she and Harris shared the same taste in furniture, she thought as she ran her hand over the sofa's tufted back.

"Have a seat," he said. "It will only take me a second to light the fire. It's gas."

As Sofia sat down, she eyed the curated selection of books stacked neatly on top of the large coffee table that stood in the center of the room—books about art, architecture and photography, as if chosen for someone who appreciated luxury.

The whoosh of the fire starting made her look up. Rather than traditional logs, the base of the firebox was filled with shimmering clear-glass beads that reflected the blue light from the fire, creating a dynamic, sparkling effect as the flames flickered.

He sat beside her, close enough that their knees touched. "I mentioned I had another surprise," he said, his voice soft and full of anticipation, unlike when they'd spoken about Linc. "Are you up for an adventure?"

"That depends."

"Last night, I was serious when I said that sometimes you just have to stop overthinking things and take the leap. Let's go to Paris, Sofia. I've already made arrangements—we're here so I can pack a bag. Jacinta's at your house packing a bag for you as we speak. I talked to her early this morning."

She gasped. "You did?"

"Yes," he answered smoothly. "Not only has she agreed to be on standby in case Dan and the kids need something while we're gone, but she's agreed to pick them up in Waco on Wednesday and keep them until we get back. I thought we could stay a week. You're right—for your first trip, you do need to do more than a fly-by. Jacinta thinks I'm going to propose."

He laughed, but Sofia was paralyzed. Was he really backing her into a corner?

"You didn't tell her we're already married, did you?"

"No, of course not." He reached over and tenderly stroked her cheek. "But this could be our honeymoon, Sofia, and when we come back from Paris, we could tell people we're married. We could just skip the details about the ceremony happening in Vegas."

Honeymoon? She was still processing this impromptu Vegas wedding, and here he was, fast-tracking them to a life in which each card revealed seemed farther and farther away from what she wanted.

Clearly, he didn't understand her as well as she thought he did.

"Whoa, slow down." Her words sounded as if they'd come from outside of herself. Her breath hitched, and her heart galloped, the precursor to a panic attack. She tried to draw in a breath, but the air didn't fill her lungs.

"This is...a lot."

The smile on Harris's face faltered. He looked at her, concern flickering in his eyes. "Talk to me," he said gently. "Tell me what's going on in that beautiful head of yours."

Sofia set her coffee on the table, her hands trembling. "I can't just leave my kids and go to Paris. I have clients—and responsibilities. I can't just drop everything, Harris."

He leaned forward, his expression soft but determined. "Sofia, it's just a week. Jacinta has everything covered. She's going to take care of the kids and ask Heather to reschedule your clients at the salon. You deserve this."

He took her hand, but she pulled away.

"No." Her voice firmer. "That's not how I do things. I don't just abandon my life to fly off somewhere on a whim. You're thinking of Paris as our honeymoon, but you don't seem to realize that I haven't ruled out the annulment."

"We said we were going to try and make things work."

"I did say that, but I also didn't say dissolving the marriage was off the table."

"Sofia," he pleaded, reaching for her hand, but she pulled away. "Trust me."

And that was the problem.

How could she trust him when she didn't trust *herself*? She had fallen hard for Dan, too, once upon a time. She'd trusted him. Look where that had gotten her.

Her voice was soft but resolute. "This isn't real life, Harris. This…" She waved her hand around at the opulent surroundings. "It's not my life."

His face darkened. "What are you saying?"

"I'm saying," she replied carefully, "this is too much. You and I live in different worlds. Our lives don't fit."

The weight of her words settled between them, heavy and insurmountable.

"I'm sorry, Harris," she whispered. "This is such a nice gesture, but I can't. I need to go. Please take me home?"

The silence in the car on the way home was thick with tension. All she could think about was that he had assumed this would be fine; he'd taken it for granted, but he hadn't asked her how she felt about it. Actually, he had. Last night, they'd talked about Paris, and she'd made her position clear, which meant he hadn't heard her.

That made it even worse.

He finally broke the silence as they pulled up to her house. "Let's talk about this. I want to make this work."

"Really? Why? You think you have me all figured out, but you don't even know me, Harris."

He turned to her, eyes burning with sincerity. "I feel like I've known you forever."

He thumped a fist over his heart.

"I'll bet you didn't know this about me," Sofia said. "I'm not sure I want more children. I don't want to be the reason you never have children of your own. Mostly, I don't want you to grow resentful of me because I didn't give you children."

She let the words hang in the air before continuing.

"I'm sorry, but I have to ask about Amanda."

"What about her?" Harris said thickly.

"You were ready to walk down the aisle and you didn't know she didn't want kids. How did you not know this about the woman you were going to spend the rest of your life with?"

"It's not as if kids dominated the conversation. We talked about it. She lied to me and told me she wanted kids. I took her at her word."

"Did you talk to Amanda about what *she* wanted, or did you just hear what you wanted to hear? Did you ask her why she didn't want kids? Maybe there was a reason. Maybe you had a version of her in your head that you wanted to be true, and it blinded you."

"Wow, that's harsh." His knuckles tightened on the steering wheel.

"I'm sorry," Sofia said, "but if we're even going to consider making this marriage work, we need to ask the hard questions and talk about difficult things. Because from where I sit, it sounds like you didn't know Amanda as well as you thought you did."

"You have no idea about that relationship," he gritted out.

"You're right, but I do know that you don't know me well enough to say that you want to spend the rest of your life with me. Because, Harris, I wouldn't mind being married again... someday. But next time, it's going to last."

Chapter Thirteen

On Wednesday night, Harris sat on his veranda, sipping a bourbon on the rocks and staring at the sunset and the long shadows the fading light cast across the lawn.

Sofia and the kids would've been home from Waco by now. He itched to call her but now wasn't the time. She and Kaitlin and Jackson would have a lot of catching up to do after being away from each other this week.

He and Sofia hadn't spoken since Monday afternoon when he'd dropped her off at her house after the Paris dispute. Before he'd left, he told her to call him when she was ready to talk.

And, well, here it was Wednesday evening, and there had been nothing but radio silence.

While he wasn't upset with her, he did feel conflicted.

Maybe she was right? Maybe they were too different? He'd had a lot of time to think about it, and all roads had him coming back to how right they were for each other.

He hadn't meant to come on so strong. He'd only wanted to shake her out of her comfort zone and get her to Paris. It had seemed like an exciting adventure. A chance for them to spend time together outside of Emerald Ridge. He'd gotten caught up in the romance of sweeping her off her feet and whisking her away.

Sure, a part of him had hoped to help her realize it was

okay to let go a little. It was like coaxing someone to jump off a high dive for the first time. Sure, it was scary, but with him there, holding her hand, he'd hoped she could do it. In retrospect, he realized that it must've been a bit overwhelming for her to make that leap. He could see now that he'd pushed too hard, too fast.

That's why he'd given her some space to breathe. Even though he hadn't wanted her to feel crowded, Tuesday and Wednesday, while she was at work, he'd gone over to her house and finished building the tree house and balance beam for the kids. No matter what happened between Sofia and him, he would keep his promise to Jackson and Kaitlin.

She must've been picking up on his vibe because his phone sounded a notification and the incoming text was from her.

Harris's stomach knotted as the selfie that he'd snapped of them glowed on his lock screen.

Hi, Harris. I hope you're doing well. I'm home with the kids. Thank you for all your hard work on the tree house and balance beam. The kids are exhausted and having an early bedtime, which means they haven't seen the beam and tree house yet. I'm taking Thursday and Friday off since they go back to school on Monday. I was wondering if you'd like to come over tomorrow morning for the big unveiling?

The next morning, Harris stood on Sofia's deck, smiling as Kaitlin and Jackson raced around the yard, looking at what he had built for them. There were whoops of delight as they took it all in—the sturdy wooden platform nestled high in the oak tree, and the balance beam stretching across the lawn.

The beam sat low to the ground, but Harris had made it adjustable so it could be raised as the girl's skills and confidence improved.

"Wow!" Kaitlin shrieked as she walked toe-to-heel on the apparatus. "I can't believe I have my very own balance beam!"

Jackson followed behind his sister, his arms outstretched like airplane wings, trying to keep his balance.

"This is so cool," he murmured, his concentration fierce as he carefully placed one foot in front of the other.

Kaitlin jumped down and ran to the tree house, where she climbed the wooden ladder, giggling as she pulled herself up onto the platform. "Jackson, come up here," she called down, peeking out from one of the windows Harris had cut into the walls. "It's like our own little fort!"

Harris had half expected the kids to place ownership on the new play structures and he was pleased by how well they were sharing them. He watched them with a sense of pride that ran deeper than he'd expected. They were such good kids. Harris's heart twisted as he realized how much he would miss them if things didn't work out with Sofia. His gaze wandered to the bed-swing where they'd made love on Sunday, and a mixture of sadness and longing tugged at his insides.

How can I make this right?

He knew the only thing he could do was to be here for Sofia and let time run its course. The ten-day agreement officially ended today. Even though the original plan had been interrupted, he wasn't going to ask her to extend it.

"They love it," Sofia said, coming up behind him. Her voice was soft and a little hesitant, but the gratitude was clear in her tone.

"I'm glad they do. It was a lot of fun putting everything together. I don't get to do projects like that as much as I'd like to."

"How did you learn to do all this?" she asked, making an

all-encompassing gesture that included the deck, beam and tree house.

"It all started in high school shop class and it became a hobby. Some people paint, some play tennis and golf. I like woodworking. But I do like golf and tennis, too."

"If you ever need a recommendation, you've got one."

Kaitlin popped her head out of the tree house and shouted down, "Mr. Harris, are we still going horseback riding today? You promised if I didn't ride the ponies at the fall festival, we could ride horses when I got back from Daddy's house."

Harris glanced at Sofia. "I did promise that, didn't I?"

"Harris, you don't have to."

"I don't like to break promises," he said.

Sofia inhaled, and even though she didn't move, Harris felt her take a step away from him. "It's sweet of you to offer, but…"

She trailed off and he sensed that she was about to say, *It's not in the budget.*

"It would be on the house, of course," he preempted.

Sofia squinted at him. Even though she didn't mention it, he knew she was wondering *why.*

"Aaron Walsh and I have done business in the past. I can call in a favor." Before she could protest further, he quickly added, "It wouldn't cost a thing, and it would be a nice way to spend the afternoon. How about it? I think the kids would love it."

Playfully, she swatted him on the arm. "You are too persuasive for your own good." Their gazes caught, and for a moment, it felt like things were shifting back in the right direction.

She looked away and murmured, "Too persuasive for *my* own good."

"Do you ride?" he asked, trying to get the conversation back on neutral ground.

Her pensive look transformed into a grimace. "Me? No, I've never been on a horse in my life."

"Well, there's a first time for everything. You can take a lesson, too."

Sofia raised an eyebrow and started to speak, but he beat her to it. "You might as well. It's available to you, but it's up to you."

She studied him for a moment, a look of gratitude on her face. "Thank you, Harris. I know the kids will have such a good time."

In companionable silence, they watched the children play for a while longer, their laughter filling the morning air. Eventually, Harris cleared his throat. "I got a call from Cathy Henderson's office this morning," he said, keeping his voice neutral. "She's back from vacation. She offered us an appointment for Monday morning at eleven o'clock. What do you think?"

Sofia's smile faltered, a flicker of sadness crossing her face. "I think we should talk to her," she said quietly.

Harris's heart squeezed in his chest. He nodded, trying to keep his own emotions in check. "Okay. I'll confirm it with her assistant."

At Walsh Equestrian Estate, the kids were virtually vibrating with excitement as they geared up for their first riding lesson. Harris watched as the trainer helped Kaitlin onto a gentle mare, her face lighting up with pure joy. Jackson was already in the paddock astride an Appaloosa.

Sofia looked a little unsure, her gaze darting from one child to the other. She had been quiet after he'd brought up the appointment with the lawyer, but what was there to talk about? He didn't want it, but she did and he'd promised that he would grant her the annulment at the end of their time together if she still wanted it. He would follow through and see what was involved in getting an annulment so they could weigh their options.

"I can't believe I'm doing this," she murmured as she watched another instructor approaching with a beautiful chestnut Morgan.

"You're going to be great," Harris assured her.

"I'll trust you," she said.

Her words were bittersweet.

Finally, he thought. But it sort of felt like it was too little too late.

After she was astride the horse, Aaron Walsh approached. "Harris, good to see you, buddy. Can I have a word?"

Sofia and the kids were already immersed in the lesson. Harris nodded. "Sure."

Aaron walked along the edge of the paddock away from the lesson. "I've been wanting to talk to you about something," he said, his tone low. "It's about Linc."

Harris's chest tightened at the mention of his old friend. "What about him?" he asked, his voice careful.

Aaron hesitated, his gaze shifting downward at his dusty boots before gazing over Harris's shoulder rather than looking him in the eyes. "I didn't think it was anything at the time, but I saw Linc arguing with someone at the park. Not sure of the exact date…maybe late July? It was not long before he… you know. Anyway, I wasn't sure if I should even mention it."

Harris's pulse quickened. "What do you mean? What kind of argument?"

Aaron shrugged. "I couldn't hear them, but it looked heated. You know, Linc was always a pretty calm guy, but that day he seemed agitated, and the other guy—well, I didn't get a good look at him. It was from a distance, but he didn't seem very happy either."

A dozen impatient quips ran through Harris's head, such as, 'And you're just coming forward with this now, three months later?' But aggression wouldn't help. It might spook Aaron and make him clam up.

Harris chose his words wisely. "Do you remember anything about the guy Linc was arguing with? What he looked like? What he was wearing?"

Aaron shook his head. "Not really. It was just a glance. But I thought…maybe it's worth mentioning to the police? I don't want to cause any trouble if it's nothing, but…"

Harris placed a hand on the man's shoulder. "You should tell them. Absolutely. Even if it seems small, something like this could be a piece of the puzzle that leads the police to the killer or at least gives them a clue. Please, Aaron, tell the police everything you remember."

Aaron nodded, though his expression remained uneasy. "I'll give them a call today."

As Harris watched him walk away, a sense of dread crept into his chest. Linc's murder had left a gaping hole in his life, but if Aaron's memory could help solve it, then maybe there was still hope for justice. He turned his gaze back to the paddock, where Sofia and the kids were laughing and seeming to have the time of their lives. A strange mixture of sadness and longing washed over him once again.

A realization broke through the melancholic haze. Life was short. Too short for Linc. You weren't promised more on this earth than the breath you were drawing right now. Harris was glad he'd stayed in Emerald Ridge instead of going back to Dallas. If he had, Aaron might never have mentioned the argument.

And Harris might not have gotten to know Sofia.

However, Monday was coming. The appointment with the divorce attorney loomed like a shadow. It was finally clear to him that he was in love with Sofia. Why had he wasted so much time ignoring these feelings? Maybe it was self-preservation since she wasn't ready to be married again. He could see it in her eyes. Because he loved her, he would give her the space she needed. He wouldn't force her into a life she wasn't ready to embrace.

On Monday morning, as Sofia walked toward the entrance of Cathy Henderson's Dallas law office, her aching heart grew heavier as she spied Harris standing outside waiting for her. Arms crossed, he wore a solemn expression on his handsome face. As soon as he saw Sofia, a smile flickered across his lips, but it didn't quite reach his eyes.

She hesitated for a moment. A rush of conflicting emotions surged through her. Part of her wanted to call off this meeting. But she couldn't; they needed to explore all the options.

Harris clearly cared for her kids. He adored them in ways that made her heart ache because it reminded her of what she longed for—stability, a real family again. But could she give him what he needed? Could she be the kind of wife he deserved?

"Morning," Harris said as she came to a stop in front of him. He leaned in, brushing a kiss against her cheek. The familiar scent of leather and sandalwood swept over her, stirring memories that left her both comforted and unsettled. She fought the instinct to turn her face toward him and kiss his lips.

"Good morning." She forced a smile. They stood there, looking at each other. For a moment, she wondered if he was having second thoughts, too. But they owed it to each other to at least hear what the attorney had to say.

"Shall we?" Harris opened the door for and her she stepped into the cool, quiet office. The air smelled faintly of copier fluid and floor polish.

The receptionist took their names, placed a phone call and finally walked them back to Cathy's office.

She greeted them from behind her desk. With her sleek, chestnut-colored hair pulled into a low bun and her tailored suit, she appeared to be a no-nonsense woman. Sofia guessed that she was in her mid-forties.

"Hello." She stood and offered her hand as she introduced herself, assessing them with her sharp gaze. "Please have a seat, and we'll get started."

The way she commanded the meeting made it clear that she didn't waste time with frivolities.

Sofia glanced at Harris before settling into the leather chair across from Cathy's imposing desk. Harris followed suit. The space between them seemed miles wider than the few inches that separated their chairs.

Cathy donned a pair of reading glasses and opened a file. "So, you're seeking an annulment," she began, glancing between the two of them. Before they had a chance to answer, she continued, "I'll be honest—annulments aren't easy to obtain. It's not simply a matter of regret or wishing something hadn't happened. There are specific legal grounds that must be met before this can happen. Please tell me about the circumstances of your marriage?"

Sofia shifted in her seat, feeling like an idiot, before uttering the first word. "We…we spent one drunken night together in Las Vegas and woke up married." Her voice was tight. "I would not have consented if I'd been sober."

She kept her gaze pinned on Cathy because she couldn't bear to look at Harris. The woman tapped her pen against the desk. "I see. And can you prove that you were intoxicated at the time?"

Sofia blinked. "*Prove* it?"

"Yes. Any witnesses? Photographs? Videos? Wedding footage, for instance. If there are videos or photos of the ceremony, they could show signs of intoxication—slurred speech, stumbling, or anything that suggests you were not in full control of your faculties. Do you have anything like that?"

"We, uh…" Sofia glanced at Harris.

"We didn't have a big ceremony," he said. "It was a quick and spur-of-the-moment exchange of vows. No one else was there."

Cathy raised an eyebrow. "No witnesses at all?"

He shook his head. "Only the chapel employees. It was late, and we didn't know anyone there. Alcohol was involved, and we didn't think it through."

The attorney leaned back in her chair. "Well, we could still use other evidence. Pre-wedding and post-wedding footage, if you have any. Photos or videos from before and after the ceremony, especially from bars or celebrations. Do you have anything like that to show how intoxicated you were leading up to the event?"

They hadn't taken any photos. Suddenly, Sofia remembered someone at the wedding chapel snapping a photo, but the picture hadn't made it back to the hotel.

Clearly taking their silence as a no, Cathy asked, "Any receipts? Did you have a bar tab showing the amount of alcohol consumed? Or do you have credit card statements documenting alcohol purchases?"

"I have a receipt for the purchase of two drinks at a club where we went dancing before the ceremony," Harris said. "Our dinner, which had wine pairings, was where we consumed most of the alcohol. It was comped. A friend of mine owns the restaurant. I guess we could ask him to vouch for us."

Sofia groaned, burying her face in her hands. "Which means we'll have to tell him we're married. I didn't want anyone else to know."

Cathy nodded, her expression sympathetic but firm. "It might be your best bet. As it stands, we don't have much to go on."

She paused and shuffled through some pages in the file. "You said you woke up married. Not to be indelicate, but was the relationship consummated?"

Cathy's tone was matter-of-fact, but Sofia felt heat creep up her neck. She glanced at Harris, who looked equally uncomfortable.

"Yes," he said.

"Have you been intimate since returning to…" She glanced at the file. "Emerald Ridge?"

"Yes," he said, again.

Cathy nodded. "That complicates things. Courts are less likely to grant annulments when the marriage was consummated, especially if it happened after the marriage took place."

Sofia frowned, her thoughts swirling. She hadn't expected this to be easy, but she hadn't realized it would be this humiliating.

"I wouldn't have gotten married in Vegas like that if I'd been in my right mind," she insisted.

Harris cleared his throat, his voice soft but steady. "Would you have married me otherwise?"

The question caught her off guard. She turned to look at him, her heart skipping a beat. "What?"

"I'm asking," he said, holding her gaze, "if the circumstances had been different—if we hadn't been drunk and I'd proposed—would you have married me?"

Sofia's mind went blank for a moment. The answer seemed obvious, didn't it? "Harris… I didn't even know you then. And if it weren't for this…" She motioned between them. "We might not know each other now."

Harris cocked an eyebrow, a small smile tugging at the corners of his lips. "Exactly. Drunken marriage or not, I don't hate that I met you. In fact, if anything good has come out of it, it's that."

The weight of his words settled over her, thick and heavy. Her chest tightened as emotions warred inside her. This wasn't what she had planned, not any of it. But Harris…he had become something more than an impulsive mistake. He had become a part of her life. Of her kids' lives.

Cathy cleared her throat, bringing them back to the present. "I'm sorry, but do you or don't you want to annul this marriage?"

Sofia's first thought was, *No!* The word clanged against her heart, the clapper against the steel of a bell. But what fell from her lips was, "Yes." It slipped out before she could stop it, clashing against Harris's quiet but emphatic, "No."

The room fell silent, the weight of their responses muddying the waters like a thick fog. Sofia's pulse thrummed in her ears, and she wanted nothing more than to take back that errant *yes*. But her answer was out, and she couldn't undo it.

Cathy sighed and removed her readers. Her gaze softened. "I must inform you that if this exchange happened in front of a judge, there's no way he or she would grant an annulment. If you both aren't sure, I'd advise you to take some time to think about it before we proceed."

Sofia glanced at Harris, her heart heavy with the weight of the situation. She could feel his sadness rolling off him in waves. It echoed her own, but she didn't know how to make this right.

Cathy closed the file and folded her hands on top of it. "Look, I can start the paperwork, but I'm sensing some hesitancy on your part as well, Ms. Gomez Simon. My advice? Don't rush into this if you're not completely certain."

Sofia stared down at her hands, at the bare ring finger on her left hand. The wedding ring Harris had bought her was in her jewelry box at home. Her mind was spinning. Was this really what she wanted? She wasn't sure anymore. She wasn't sure of anything.

"This will sound like I'm contradicting myself since I told you not to rush into it," Cathy said. "If you do want to go through with it, time is of the essence. I need affidavits from both of you about your state of mind, how much you drank, and your memories of what led to the event. Also, I will need testimony from your restauranteur friend, Mr. Fortune." Cathy paused, and when she spoke again, her voice was softer. "Sometimes, the hardest part isn't admitting the mistake. It's deciding whether or not you want to fix it."

Sofia swallowed hard, her heart aching. For the first time since they'd woken up married in Vegas, she wasn't sure if *fixing it* meant undoing it—or finding a way to make it work.

Chapter Fourteen

Harris was not having a good day. For that matter, he hadn't had a good day since he and Sofia had argued about Paris and decided to put some distance between them. Since then, it had all been one big blur of bad.

Today had been particularly challenging because he'd finally bitten the bullet and outlined exactly what he needed to say to Carl Woodward when he reached out to ask him to attest to the amount of alcohol he and Sofia had consumed at his restaurant, Laurel.

Harris had written down everything he needed from Carl, but he just couldn't bring himself to send the email.

It had been three days since they'd met with Cathy Henderson, and he needed to send the message before the end of the day.

But first, lunch.

Stepping away would allow him to clear his head and come back with better focus. Then he'd read through it one more time and send it off. He ignored the way his stomach churned, blaming it on hunger.

Harris got into his car and headed downtown. Since he and Sofia were giving each other space, he'd been avoiding that part of town because her salon was there and he didn't want her to think he was stalking her. But today, he felt restless. His house seemed too quiet, too big, with nothing to do but think.

He had attempted to read a business proposal. The third time he reached the bottom of the page and realized that he had no idea what he'd read, he knew something had to change. He needed to get out of his head because his mind was a fog of memories and regrets.

He couldn't live this way.

Harris vowed that after he grabbed a bite to eat and sent off the request to Carl, he would get himself together.

Francesca's Bar and Grill was just what the doctor ordered. Their specialty, the cowboy burger—with its double patties, cheddar and pepper jack cheese, bacon, onion straws and generous slather of BBQ sauce—was the perfect medicine.

It was early, so the lunch crowd hadn't yet descended. He took a seat at the bar, which was virtually empty except for Jesse, the bartender, who took his order.

While Harris waited, he glanced around the place—at the earth-tone décor, stone walls and wooden accents. He eyed the few occupied tables he could see from where he sat, hoping he'd see Sofia, but she wasn't there.

The last bite of the burger had been satisfying, but it hadn't filled the hollowness gaping in Harris's chest. He guessed he wouldn't feel whole again until the matter of their marriage was settled. He tossed some bills that included a generous tip on the bar and resolved to man-up and do what he needed to do.

Harris left the bar and grill. The sound of clinking plates and murmured conversations faded behind him. As he stepped onto the sidewalk that boarded the bustling Emerald Ridge Boulevard, the bracing October wind cut through him. He zipped his jacket shut. He couldn't help but glance in the direction of The Style Lounge, but then he turned in the opposite direction and headed toward his car.

Downtown, with its quaint businesses and shops, was alive

with its usual vibrant buzz. A group of women spilled out of the Coffee Connection, talking and laughing, and holding festive-looking drinks. Next he saw a couple walk out of a jewelry shop holding hands. It was right next door to the florist where Harris had picked up that beautiful bouquet for Sofia. Had it really been nearly two weeks since he'd bought the flowers? In some ways, it seemed like yesterday. In others, it seemed like a lifetime ago. Despite all the life around him, Harris felt like he was moving through it in a daze.

"Harris," called a familiar female voice.

He turned and saw his sister, Zara, walking toward him. Tall, with her long blond hair flowing over her shoulders, and dressed in her usual stylishly casual way, she looked pretty as ever. But her face was lined with worry, and her green eyes were not quite as bright as they usually were.

Harris forced a smile. "Hey, Zara. What's going on?"

They hugged, and she held on to him a little longer than usual.

"I haven't seen you since the fall festival," she said. "Where have you been hiding?"

He ran a hand over his chin. "I've been around. I just finished grabbing a bite of lunch before I get back to work."

"Did you meet Sofia?"

The words sucker-punched him. If things crumbled, he'd have to address the breakup…but not right now. The best way around that was to change the subject.

"I hear Finn Morrison is back in town," he said. "Have you talked to him?"

Zara blanched and then sighed. "No. He's pretty much avoiding me."

"You okay?" Harris asked.

"Yes." His sister spit out the word, but in the next instant, she shook her head, and her green eyes welled.

"Hey, what's going on?" Harris asked, pulling her into a hug, wishing he hadn't mentioned Finn.

She stepped back and tried to blink away the unshed tears. "Look at me. I'm a mess."

He didn't know what to say.

"It's hard, Harris. I really loved him, and he broke my heart. After all these years, I thought I was over him, but…"

She shrugged.

Harris studied her face, the pain evident.

"What happened between you two?" he asked gently.

Zara's lips pressed into a thin line. "I wish I knew. One minute, we were crazy about each other, and the next…he couldn't stand to be around me, but he wouldn't tell me why. I've always suspected it was because he felt like he didn't belong. You know, he was a townie, working at the country club, and I…well, you know. We were members. I think it embarrassed him."

He frowned. "That doesn't make sense. Finn's a good guy. We never thought any less of him for working there. Hell, it was a respectable job."

Zara shrugged, but her eyes clouded over. "I know, but he told me he always felt like he was on the outside looking in." She took a deep breath and let it out slowly. "No matter what, I wish him well. I hope he's getting some answers about his missing adoption file and what might have happened to it. That whole situation with his file going missing still feels off. I hope there's nothing shady going on there."

Harris nodded. "I've been thinking about how Priscilla was wondering how the Morrisons could afford the exorbitant fees that the Texas Royale Private Adoption Agency charged. Finn's parents weren't wealthy. Do you know anything about how they managed to afford the fees when they adopted him?"

Her brows knitted together. "No idea. They were solid,

hardworking people, but definitely not rolling in money. I guess we'll never know. Finn won't even talk to me anymore. I wish there were something I could do to help him."

Harris could hear the tension in her voice, the mix of heartbreak and unresolved questions. "Well, you know I'm here if you ever need to talk about it. I hate seeing you upset."

She gave him a weak smile. "Thanks, Harris. But enough about me. How are things with Sofia?"

Harris stiffened.

"She's busy with the salon and the kids," he said, trying to keep it vague.

Zara beamed. "You two make such a cute couple. You should bring her to the next family dinner."

Harris forced a laugh. "Yeah, maybe, but I need to run." He pulled his sister in for another hug, not wanting her to see the sadness in his eyes. "Talk to you later."

He walked toward his car, the weight of the day pressing down on him. Everything was unraveling, and no matter how hard he tried, he couldn't fix it.

"Harris?"

This time, his cousin, Kelsey, called his name. She was just coming out of Emerald Ridge Camera and Photo, holding a small envelope.

"Hey, Kelsey," he said, offering a tired smile.

"I'm glad I ran into you. What are you up to?"

"Just had lunch at Francesca's." Harris nodded toward the photo shop. "Were you able to find out anything? Did they have any record of my parents getting a bunch of photos framed?"

Kelsey shook her head. "I wish I had better news. Unfortunately, their records don't go that far back."

He had been holding out hope that the framing shop might provide a solid lead about the "surprise" his parents had left for him and his siblings. But they had reached another dead end.

"Well, thanks for checking anyway," he said glumly.

"I'd been meaning to get in there sooner, but the ranch has kept me busy."

"How are things going over there?" he asked. "Has the situation improved any since the last time we talked?"

Kelsey shifted her weight from one foot to the other. "It's about the same, I guess. I still have several jobs that need good, reliable people. If you know any team players, please let me know. How's Sofia? I haven't seen her around much."

All these questions about his wife.

Even though he hadn't realized it until now, this was the reason he hadn't been out much since things had gone south with Sofia. He tried to keep his expression neutral and employed the same words he'd used with Zara.

"She's busy."

Kelsey studied him, her eyes narrowing slightly. "You two doing okay?"

Harris plastered on another fake smile. "Yeah, everything's fine. It's great."

But his cousin wasn't buying it. She tilted her head, her expression softening. "You know, Harris, if you ever need to talk, I'm here."

The truth was, he didn't know how to talk about what was happening with Sofia. He didn't know how to explain the slow unraveling of something that had such potential, even though he never really had her to begin with.

Maybe the fact that he didn't know how to discuss it was why everything was coming undone.

"Thanks, Kelse," he said, his voice rougher than he intended. "I appreciate it."

After he got to his car, he sat there for a moment, staring

into the middle distance. If he didn't learn how to communicate, he was going to lose Sofia.

He wasn't going to let that happen.

Sofia stood at her station in The Style Lounge, staring blankly into the middle distance of the silver-framed mirror in front of her. Her next two clients had canceled. The salon was quiet, save for the soft hum of a blow dryer and the distant murmur of a conversation happening near the front desk. She wasn't sure how long she'd been holding the comb that was in her hand. She'd meant to sanitize it, but her mind was miles away, tangled up in thoughts of Harris.

Today was Thursday. They hadn't spoken since Monday. She had tried—truly tried—not to think about him. She'd thrown herself into work, scheduled back-to-back appointments, and ensured she was too busy to let her thoughts wander to him. Yet here she was, distracted beyond reason, unable to concentrate on the simplest of tasks.

How could she still be unsure? Usually, she knew exactly what she wanted, but here she was, second-guessing herself at every turn.

She'd woken up this morning with a ridiculous idea. She had said a prayer that if she and Harris were supposed to be together, the heavens would send her a sign today. She'd hoped, foolishly perhaps, that Harris would call or text, something to pull her out of this limbo. She glanced at her phone, lying on the black-marble counter at her station.

No missed calls.

No texts.

No signs.

The silence was deafening, and with each passing hour, she grew more despondent.

Even though the canceled appointments had left her with

too much time to stew in her own uncertainty, it was probably a good thing the clients had rescheduled.

It was probably Heaven's way of telling her she wasn't fit for human interaction right now and needed to get her act together.

She plunked the purple comb into the Barbicide container and gave herself a mental shake. She didn't want to go home because she had two more clients later that afternoon, but she needed to do something constructive.

Sofia supposed she could go downstairs to the basement and do inventory, but she'd be too alone with her thoughts down there.

Company sounded better. She glanced around. Her coworkers were busy and would be tied up for a while.

Besides, they'd just talk shop. Sofia needed something... more.

She could go out and get something to eat, but she wasn't hungry. Coffee would be nice. In the next instant, she found herself calling up her cousin's number. Jacinta was married to a Fortune. Sofia knew that just because they shared the same name and vast family, the Fortune men weren't a one-size-fits-all design. Still, Jacinta seemed so happy since she and Micah had gotten married, almost like a different person.

Like a woman in love.

If one believed in such a notion.

Sofia's heart twisted at the thought.

Jacinta picked up on the second ring.

"Are you busy?" Sofia asked.

"What's going on?" Jacinta said. "Are you okay? You sound..."

"I don't know. I need to talk to you."

"Marisol will be here in thirty minutes for her shift. Then I can come by. Hang tight."

A half hour felt like an eternity, but it was good of her cousin to make the time.

In the meantime, Sofia decided to tackle the inventory. There was no cell reception downstairs, which meant she'd have no reason to check her phone every five minutes.

She texted Jacinta.

I'll be in the salon's basement. Bring coffee.

Jacinta texted back.

Yes, my queen. How else may I serve you?

The basement was cool and smelled faintly of shampoo and hair dye, a familiar and oddly comforting scent. Sofia walked over to the shelves where she kept the supplies and started counting bottles of conditioner, noting which dyes needed to be reordered, and then double-checking because her mind was chaos and she couldn't focus.

Jacinta knew that she and Harris were *involved*. But she didn't know the entire story.

How much should she tell her?

Living with Harris had been…intense. More so than she'd anticipated. It had only been for a little while—and he'd stayed in the casita all but one night—but in that short time, it felt like an entire lifetime had unfolded between them.

They'd had breakfast together as a family every morning and dinner in the evenings. He'd helped the kids with their homework and read them bedtime stories. He was so sweet with them. They'd sat on the couch together after the kids had gone to bed…just being. It had been as close to domestic bliss as she'd ever experienced.

But therein was the problem.

Harris was the kind of guy who wanted an adventurous woman who could drop everything at a moment's notice and jet off to exotic places.

In theory, she wished she could be the woman he needed, but she wasn't. Sofia was the mother of two young children. She owned a thriving business and served clients who depended on her to help them look their best. And she couldn't make a habit of rescheduling appointments because Harris wanted her to jet off to Paris on the spur of the moment.

She was successful at running a salon and doing hair because it was systematic work. Sure, it was creative, but the heart and soul of it ran on a schedule. There wasn't a lot of wiggle room for rearranging things at the last minute.

But the other truth—the one that seemed to override everything else—was that she had fallen for Harris. She'd fallen *hard*.

She was in love with him.

He had proved himself right. He had shown her that love was real. The problem was, love was also fleeting and wouldn't last.

"Why are you hiding in the basement?" Jacinta materialized at the bottom of the steps, holding two cups of coffee from the Emerald Ridge Café.

Sofia turned to her, and Jacinta drew in a breath when she saw her face. "Oh, honey, you'd better sit down and tell me everything."

They sat next to each other on the bottom step. Sofia swallowed one fortifying sip of her coffee, opened her mouth and the words started pouring out: Meeting Harris in Vegas. Accepting his invitation to dinner after she'd received Jacinta's text with the photo of Dan and the blonde. The dinner, dancing, kissing in front of the Eiffel Tower on the Vegas Strip and waking up…married.

"I'm in love with him, Jacinta, but—"

Sofia held up a hand and shook her head because deep down, she knew it was a recipe for disaster.

"I love him, and I'm terrified." A tear rolled down her cheek and she swiped it away with the back of her hand.

"You love him, and it's pretty clear that he loves you, too," Jacinta murmured. "What are you afraid of?"

Sofia shrugged. "We come from such different worlds—"

"Opposites attract," Jacinta stated in that cocksure way of hers that usually irritated Sofia to the core. Right now, however, she wanted nothing more than for her know-it-all cousin to be right.

But it wasn't that easy.

She inhaled a shuttering breath. "I know this will sound weird, but the way we rushed into it, the situation feels eerily similar to how things went with Dan."

Jacinta gave Sofia the side-eye. "That makes absolutely no sense. I mean, come on. In what world could that be true?"

Sofia waved Jacinta's skepticism away. "It's hard to explain."

"Well, yeah, because it *doesn't* make sense. Dan was your first and only love—until now. Dan is…" Jacinta pursed her lips and moved her head from side to side as if weighing her words.

"I know Dan could be a jerk. And on the surface he and Harris are as different as night and day." Sofia swallowed a lump in her throat. "But I jumped headfirst into marriage with Dan without facing the reality that we wanted different things. Dan didn't want a career woman. He wanted someone more traditional. Essentially, he wanted me to be there for him when he wanted me there."

"Yeah, and he wanted to go out drinking with his buddies the rest of the time."

"That's not entirely true, Jacinta. But it's not the point. Harris loves the idea of me as a successful businesswoman, and he can be down-to-earth in so many ways, but I can't lose sight of who he really is." She threw up her hands in exasperation. "The guy has a private plane, for heaven's sake! He's used to jetting off to Paris or wherever he pleases at a moment's notice."

"So…" Jacinta prodded.

"So the point is, I'm not *that* woman. I can't just pick up and go. My life is rooted here, in Emerald Ridge, with my kids and my salon. My kids are my world, and I'll always put them first. The world is Harris's…oyster with caviar and champagne."

Jacinta snort-laughed.

"Stop laughing," Sofia said.

"Sorry, I just—" Jacinta's guffawed. Her eyes watered. "That's just such a *Sofia* thing to say. It's funny. What does that even mean, the world is his oyster?"

Sofia stood up. "If you're going to make fun of me, just go. I don't need that right now."

Jacinta sobered. "I'm sorry. Really."

Sofia lowered herself onto the step beside her cousin again, and the two sat there in silence for a minute.

Soon, her cousin leaned into Sofia, bumping her shoulder with her own.

"You okay now?"

Sofia shrugged.

"What I was trying to say is look where ignoring the signs with Dan had got me. Divorced, with two kids who are still confused about why their father has moved out."

Her kids. That was the crux of it all, wasn't it?

"Harris is so good with them, and they love him." Sofia sighed as if the weariness of the world was bottled up inside of her. "They adore Harris, and the last thing I want is for them to become attached to someone else who might not stick around."

Jacinta nodded. "So you're willing to let a good guy—a man who is clearly in love with you—get away because you're afraid of losing him. Mmm."

Jacinta's words hung in the air, raw and…true.

"It's not that easy," she huffed. "I just can't justify the risk."

Jacinta put her arm around Sofia. "Nothing in life worth having is ever easy. You just need to decide if the risk is worth the reward."

Chapter Fifteen

As Harris started to steer his car onto Emerald Ridge Boulevard, his phone rang.

Remaining in the parking space, he hit the brakes and answered with a gruff, "Harris Fortune."

"Hello, Mr. Fortune, this is Abby Phillips. I'm the clinic nurse at Emerald Ridge Elementary School."

The kids... His heart lurched, and he braced himself for whatever news would follow.

"I have Jackson Simon in the clinic." The nurse's voice was calm, but Harris detected an undercurrent of concern. "He says he doesn't feel well. He is running a fever. So we think it would be best if someone picked him up so he could rest more comfortably and possibly see a pediatrician if need be. We have tried to reach Ms. Gomez Simon, but the calls keep going to voicemail. You are the next emergency contact on the list. Can you come to the school and pick up Jackson?"

"I'll be there in ten minutes."

The nurse's thank-you was cut off as Harris ended the call and tossed his phone onto the passenger seat. He revved the engine and sped toward the school. A fever wasn't always a big deal, he reminded himself. Kids got fevers all the time. But the idea of Jackson feeling bad and sitting alone in a nurse's office, waiting for someone to pick him up, gnawed at Harris.

Where is Sofia?

It wasn't like her to be out of communication when she was away from the kids.

A few minutes later, Harris walked into the brightly lit school office. After he signed Jackson out for the day, the receptionist led him to the clinic, where he saw three cots lining the back wall. Jackson lay on one of them, bundled in a blanket, his face flushed, his dark hair sticking up in sweaty tufts.

"Hey, buddy," Harris said gently, crouching down beside him.

Jackson's brown eyes blinked open. "Mr. Harris?" His voice was scratchy. "Where's Mommy?"

"Mommy couldn't get away right now," Harris said, forcing a smile and keeping his tone light despite the way his stomach twisted with worry over Sofia's unexplained absence. "She'll be home as soon as she can. But I'm here. I hope that's okay."

The boy nodded weakly and let Harris help him to his feet. "You ready to go home, little man?"

Jackson leaned heavily against him as they walked out of the school and toward Harris's car. On the drive home, the boy dozed, his head resting against the window.

When they reached Sofia's house, Harris fumbled for his keys. The lock on the casita was keyed the same as the front door. Thank goodness he hadn't given it back yet.

Inside, Harris led Jackson to the family room couch, wrapping him in a soft throw blanket. The boy curled up, sniffling slightly.

"Where's Mommy?" Jackson looked up at him with drooping eyes. "You said she'd be here."

"She'll be here soon," Harris assured him. "Don't worry. Close your eyes and try to sleep. When you wake up, she'll probably be here."

Jackson nodded slowly. "Okay."

Harris went into the kitchen and got the boy a glass of water. He checked his phone again—still nothing from Sofia. He tried to ignore the tightening knot of anxiety in his gut.

"I wonder if we should call your doctor and get you set up with an appointment," Harris murmured as he sat beside Jackson on the couch and held him up as he sipped the water. "Do you know your doctor's name?"

The boy nodded and pointed to the kitchen. "Mommy keeps the numbers on the fridge."

Harris got up and walked into the kitchen, scanning the list of phone numbers Sofia had neatly written and taped to the side of the refrigerator. His eyes found the pediatrician's name and number listed after Dan's and Abuela's cell numbers. He hesitated for a moment, pondering if he should call one of them first, but what would he say?

I have no idea where Sofia is...

No, that wouldn't solve anything. It would only upset the boy if they rushed over here. Harris needed to handle things until Sofia called him back. Surely, it wouldn't be much longer.

He grabbed his phone and dialed the pediatrician's office. If Sofia didn't want to keep the appointment, she could cancel it. But at least they'd be a step closer to helping Jackson feel better if he needed to see a doctor.

The receptionist picked up on the second ring. "Emerald Ridge Pediatric Associates, how may I help you?"

"Hi, this is Harris Fortune. I'm calling about Jackson Gomez Simon. He's running a fever, and I wanted to see if the doctor could take a look at him this afternoon."

"Of course, Mr. Fortune. What's his temperature right now?"

Temperature?

The school nurse had said he had a fever but hadn't been specific.

Harris paused. "Hold on a second."

He walked back into the family room and crouched down beside Jackson. "Hey, buddy, do you know where your mom keeps the thermometer?"

Jackson pointed toward the kitchen. "In the first-aid box."

Harris opened a few cupboards and found what he was looking for. Right on top was a small forehead thermometer. He pressed it against Jackson's head, and the screen flashed 102.7. Harris's stomach dropped, but he forced a calm tone as he relayed the number to the nurse.

"That's a bit high," the woman said. "We have an opening at three thirty this afternoon. In the meantime, you can give him some fever reducer—acetaminophen or ibuprofen, whatever you have on hand."

Harris disconnected the call and found the fever reducer in the first-aid kit and measured out the correct dose. He glanced at Jackson, who was watching him with sleepy, trusting eyes, and smiled softly. "We'll get you feeling better, buddy. Don't worry."

"Thanks, Mr. Harris," Jackson mumbled and then swallowed the medicine.

Jackson turned on his side and pulled the blanket up to his chin. Harris sat beside him on the couch, rubbing his back gently. After a few moments of silence, Jackson asked, "Would you read me a story?"

Harris picked up one of the books that was on the coffee table and began to read. Before long, the child's eyelids began to droop again. His breathing slowed as he drifted toward sleep. Just as Harris was about to close the book, Jackson's voice broke the quiet.

"I love you, Mr. Harris," he murmured, his voice barely audible.

The words pierced Harris's heart. "I love you, too, buddy." His voice broke on the last word.

He wasn't just standing in for Sofia—it was more than that. Jackson didn't need to be of his own blood to feel like his son. Harris's chest tightened as he gently brushed a strand of hair from the boy's forehead. Jackson was fast asleep, his small frame rising and falling with each breath.

Suddenly, Harris realized he didn't need a child of his own to feel like a father, not when he had Jackson and Kaitlin in his life. They were all the family he needed.

But where was Sofia?

It had been nearly two hours since the school had called. Harris checked his phone again—still no missed calls. His mind raced. What if something had happened to her? What if she was in trouble and couldn't call? The thought made his heart hammer against his ribs.

He stood up slowly, careful not to wake Jackson, and dialed Sofia's number again. It went straight to voicemail. Something wasn't right. Sofia was always reachable. Even when she was busy, she found a way to respond.

He couldn't sit here and wonder. He had to know she was okay.

Harris walked into the kitchen and dialed the number for The Style Lounge. His hand tightened around the phone as he listened to the line ring. His heart thudded in his chest as each ring echoed in his ear. Finally, after what felt like an eternity, someone answered.

"Style Lounge, this is Heather. How can I help you?"

"Heather, this is Harris Fortune. I need to speak to Sofia—right now. It's an emergency. Her son is sick, and neither the school nor I have been able to reach her. Is she there?"

There was a brief pause on the other end of the line. "Oh no! She's downstairs doing inventory. Hang on, Harris. I'll go get her."

Harris exhaled sharply. The tension in his gut loosened now that he knew she was there. He glanced at Jackson, still asleep on the couch. A moment later, Sofia's voice sounded over the line, frantic and breathless.

"Harris? What's happened? Is Jackson okay?"

"Yes, everything's okay now," Harris said quickly, his tone softening to reassure her. "I didn't mean to scare you. Jackson had a fever at school, and they couldn't reach you. Since I'm on the contact list, they called me. I picked him up, and brought him home. He's sleeping right now."

Sofia's sounded shaky on the other end. "I—I'm so sorry, Harris. I was in the basement doing inventory, and I left my phone in the office. I can't believe I did that."

"It's okay," he said gently. "I'm with him. I called the pediatrician and made an appointment for later this afternoon, but if you think it's not necessary, you can cancel it. I just wanted to make sure we had that option in case you wanted to take him in."

"Oh, Harris, thank you," Sofia said, her voice thick with emotion. "I can't believe I missed the call. You're amazing for taking care of him like this."

"Don't you worry about it," Harris replied, his own anxiety subsiding at the relief in her voice. "I'm just glad I could help. He's doing fine, but come home when you can."

"I'll be right there," Sofia said tearfully. "Thank you again, Harris. I'm leaving now. I'll be home in ten minutes."

"Drive safe," he said, his voice low and comforting. "We'll be here."

As he ended the call, Harris stood in the quiet of the kitchen, looking back at Jackson curled up on the couch.

He knew at that moment that no matter what happened between him and Sofia, he would always be there for her kids. That bond had already been forged, stronger than he'd ever imagined.

Sofia sat curled up on the couch, sipping a mug of herbal tea and processing everything that had happened today.

Jackson was fine. He was asleep in his bed. His fever, which had worried Sofia all afternoon, had finally broken.

Kaitlin was fine, seemingly escaping the bug that had sent her brother home from school. She was sleeping, too. As Sofia had tended to Jackson, Harris had helped Kaitlin with her homework. It was now tucked away in her backpack and ready for tomorrow.

Everything was fine...thanks, in large part, to Harris.

The realization settled over her as warm and comforting as her favorite quilt, lovingly hand-stitched by Abuela. All afternoon, she'd beaten herself up for not having her phone with her when Jackson had needed her. But she'd stopped after Harris had pointed out that mentally flogging herself wouldn't help anything.

She glanced toward the kitchen, where he was cleaning up after dinner. The smell of the Thai food he'd picked up still lingered in the air. It felt so normal, so wonderfully domestic. For a man who had entered her life like a whirlwind, Harris had found his place here effortlessly. He was good with the kids, good for her. She hadn't realized how much she needed him until tonight.

Wiping his hands on a dish towel, he looked over at her and smiled.

That smile.

She'd spent too long pushing him away, questioning everything between them, but in this moment, all she could ask herself was *why*.

Sofia didn't want him just as a backup or someone to fill in when she couldn't be there—a qualified nanny could fill that role. She wanted him because... She wanted *him*. She needed him.

She *loved* him.

And she was tired of fighting it.

So what if she'd only been divorced for three months? She needed to quit worrying about timelines and what other people might think of her moving on so fast.

Love didn't live by a schedule.

Most of all, being apart for the last few days...she'd realized that the feelings she had for him hadn't changed. If anything, they'd grown deeper and stronger as she'd understood what she'd been on the verge of throwing away.

It was time she trusted herself.

"You were wonderful today, Harris," she said, her voice thick with gratitude. "I don't know what I would've done without you."

A melancholy smile turned up the corners of his lips— those lips that had kissed her so well. Those lips she wanted to taste right now. He looked as if he wanted to say something but was weighing his words.

Sofia couldn't help but wonder what was going through his mind. Was he thinking what she was thinking? If they called off the annulment, they wouldn't have to live without each other another day.

She couldn't bring herself to say it until she was sure that's what he still wanted, too. She'd pushed him away so much. Wouldn't it be ironic if, now that she was finally figuring out her heart, she'd pushed him too far? What if he'd decided he didn't want a life with her as much as he thought he did?

It wouldn't just be ironic. It would be *devastating*.

"You certainly got a big, strong dose of life with children today," she added, her tone light. "Did it cure your *family-life fever*?"

"Fever, huh? That's an interesting choice of words." He chuckled, tossing the towel onto the counter before sitting down beside her. "I don't know. I think it only made it worse."

The butterflies fluttered in her stomach. He was teasing, but there was truth in his words. Harris had stepped up today in a way no man in her life had before. While she'd been at the doctor's with Jackson, he'd collected Kaitlin from school, helped her with her homework, and picked up dinner. After she'd gotten the kids to sleep, he'd made her a cup of tea and insisted she put her feet up while he put away the leftovers and tidied the kitchen.

He hadn't needed to do all that. After she'd rushed home from work, she'd given him an out. She'd told him Jacinta could've picked up Kaitlin. She could've managed dinner. But even after she'd pushed him away, he'd been her partner in every sense of the word today.

He'd seen her at her worst, but he'd given her his best. Not just today, but since that morning that they'd woken up married in Vegas.

His gaze softened, and that familiar warmth spread through her. She wanted to snuggle into that space next to him where she'd fit so perfectly, to touch him, to kiss him like they used to before everything had gotten so complicated. But...

Harris leaned back, studying her face as though he could sense the whirlwind of thoughts in her mind.

"The other day," he said, his voice low, "you told me that I don't know you. But I'd love the chance to prove that I do."

"I think you've already shown that you know me better than I gave you credit for, Harris. You gave me room when I needed it—" she gave her head a quick shake "—when I didn't even know what I needed… And today, you stepped up in a way that means so much to me. I can't even…"

Her voice broke, and tears welled in her eyes.

"I was honored to do it. I know you were worried that if we stayed together, I wouldn't get to have kids of my own, but one thing I realized today is how much I care about Jackson and Kaitlin. Being part of their lives would be…" He shrugged. "How could I want more? When I'm with you, Sofia, we feel like a family. You and I…we fit. Like we belong together. It's like we've known each other for lifetimes."

Her breath caught. He'd always had a way of cutting right to the heart of things. But before she could respond, he continued.

"It was a jerk move to try to pressure you to jet off to Paris without giving you time to digest it."

"I wouldn't call it a *jerk move*," she interrupted, putting a hand on his arm.

"Well, maybe not," he conceded with a small smile. "But now, I know you well enough to understand that's not how you operate."

Her heart squeezed, and feeling a little shy, she glanced up at him.

"What else do you know about me?"

"I know you love hot apple cider," he said, his smile widening, "and that you prefer Italian rosé to French, which surprised me given your love for all things French. And I know that when you're skeptical about something, you scrunch up your nose in the cutest way."

"No, I don't," she protested, though she could feel her nose scrunching up at that very moment.

He laughed and took her hand. "You're doing it right now."

She covered her face with her free hand and laughed despite herself.

Oooh.

She had missed him so much. What would she do without him?

"I know it's important to you that people listen and not just form their own opinions. I know you hated how Dan tried to control you, how it always had to be his way. I would never do that to you, Sofia. I'm sorry if it seemed that way surrounding the Paris...um...proposal."

Harris's expression grew serious. "Most of all, I learned something priceless this week. I learned that I love you, Sofia. I love you and your children more than life itself. If you don't want another baby, that's fine. It won't change how I feel about you. I want you and this family, but if you're not ready... I can wait until you are."

His voice was thick with emotion. "You're worth fighting for. I know we can make this work if you'll have me."

Her heart was pounding now. The words she'd been holding back were bubbling up inside her. Tears spilled from her eyes as she looked at him, really looked at him. How had she been so blind not to realize the man who was meant for her had been in front of her all along?

"The crazy thing is, since we've been apart, I've been asking for a sign of what to do," she confessed. "I'm realizing the big sign that the heavens sent might've been our wedding in Vegas.

"You told me to trust you," she continued, her voice trembling. "And I think, deep down, I always did. The person I didn't trust was myself. I kept waiting for something to go wrong, for everything to fall apart, because I couldn't believe it could really be this good. But I know now that if I let you go, I'm just ensuring that my trust issue becomes a self-fulfilling prophecy. I'll never find this kind of love again because I'll have let the love of my life slip away."

She paused, drawing in a shaky breath. "*You're* the love of my life, Harris. I love you, and I want us to be together."

She could see the love in Harris's eyes as he pulled her into his arms and gently brushed a tear from her cheek. He kissed her, slow and deep, as if sealing the promise they had just made. The kiss was everything she had been missing, everything she had been too afraid to admit she needed. It was full of warmth, love and certainty.

When they finally pulled apart, Harris rested his forehead against hers, his voice barely a whisper. "Earlier, you said you didn't know what you would've done without me. Don't try. Let's cancel the annulment."

Sofia's heart fluttered. "Really?"

"Really," he said. "And if you want, we could plan another wedding in Paris. In front of the real Eiffel Tower this time. But only when you're ready."

She laughed. Tears of joy in her eyes. She could picture it already—the kids would be there, Abuela, Jacinta, Micah, Harris's family—everyone they loved. The *real* Eiffel Tower, not the replica in Vegas where they'd first stumbled into marriage. This time, they would do it right. This time, it would be forever.

"I think that's a perfect plan," she whispered, leaning in to kiss him again.

As she sank into his arms, she realized something important. For years, she had been telling herself that love wasn't real, that it was just a fairy tale people told themselves to make life bearable. But she'd been wrong.

Love was real. It was right in front of her, holding her close, offering her the future she had always dreamed of but never thought she deserved.

"You, me and the kids," Harris murmured against her lips. "Forever. Do you trust me?"

"I trust you. Forever."

Epilogue

Six months later
Paris, France

The sun hung low in the April sky, casting a golden glow over the Champ de Mars. In front of Sofia, the Eiffel Tower rose majestically, its iron lattice shimmering as it reflected the last of the day's light.

The cherry blossoms that lined the grassy expanse of the park were showing off in fine fashion for a wedding. Even though she hadn't realized it before now, as she stood next to Harris getting ready to take their vows, Sofia had dreamed of this moment her entire life, never quite believing it would happen. She was finally in Paris, standing in front of the real Eiffel Tower in her wedding dress with the love of her life. Her heart was full.

Harris looked gorgeous in his black Armani tuxedo. His green eyes focused on her as if she were the only woman in the world.

"You look stunning," Harris whispered.

"You're not so bad yourself, handsome."

Sofia's heart danced as she glanced from Harris to her children. Kaitlin, her maid of honor, looked like a princess in her pretty pink-tulle dress. The girl's eyes sparkled as she beamed at her mother. Jackson was Harris's best man. He wore a cute little tux and a huge grin as the officiant welcomed everyone.

Abuela stood off to the side with Jacinta and Micah. Sofia's parents had flown in from California. Harris's family was there, too. His uncle Sander, cousin Kelsey, brother Roth and sisters, Priscilla and Zara, who both watched with tearful smiles.

It wasn't Vegas. This was the real deal. And, unlike their impulsive first ceremony, where they barely remembered the words they'd exchanged, every moment of this day would be etched on Sofia's heart.

The officiant guided them through the final part of the ceremony. When the time came to exchange their vows, Sofia handed Kaitlin her bouquet of pink cherry blossoms, white tulips and wisteria, and turned to Harris, putting her hands in his.

"I, Harris, promise to love you, Kaitlin and Jackson with all my heart for the rest of my life. You are my family, my home, and my future. My life." His voice caught, but he continued. "I promise to be there for you, no matter what the world throws at us. You just have to trust me."

Sofia laughed, letting the tears slip down her cheeks.

When it was her turn, her voice was thick with emotion. "Harris, once, I told you I didn't believe in love. I told you that marriage was just a fairy tale. I was wrong. I didn't know what real love was then, but I do now. This—what we have— it's *real*. I trust you, and I promise you, this love, this marriage, will last forever."

As the officiant pronounced them husband and wife, Harris's eyes glistened and he pulled her close. Their lips met in a gentle kiss.

Kaitlin let out a squeal of delight as she threw her arms around them both. "We're a family."

Sofia laughed, the joy washing over her in waves as she hugged her daughter back. Jackson clung to Harris, his small face buried in Harris's side. Then he looked up with wide eyes. "Does this mean you're my daddy now?"

Harris knelt, bringing himself to Jackson's level. He cupped the boy's face. "Yeah, buddy. Now, you have two dads who both love you very much."

Jackson grinned, wrapping his arms around Harris's neck in a tight hug. "I love you, Daddy."

Abuela clapped her hands. "*Ay Dios mío*, this is a special day!"

Jacinta wiped a tear from her eye, leaning against Micah's shoulder. "It's beautiful," she whispered. "They're perfect together."

After the ceremony, they all headed to Le Jules Verne, the restaurant inside the Eiffel Tower. The view was breathtaking, and the food was exquisite. Abuela couldn't stop talking about how incredible it was to be dining inside the iconic monument. Kaitlin and Jackson were in awe of everything—the sparkling lights of Paris below, the fancy dishes that arrived at their table like works of art, and the delicious chicken nuggets prepared by the chef, just for them.

As they toasted their new life together, Harris raised his champagne glass. "I'm so glad all the people who mean the most to me can be here today to help us celebrate. To family." His voice was full of emotion. "And to love."

Sofia's heart swelled as she clinked her glass against his.

As the evening came to a close, the family said goodbye. The kids were spending the night with Sofia's parents in their suite. Tomorrow, everyone except Harris and Sofia would fly home while the newlyweds stayed in Paris for their honeymoon.

When they were finally alone, standing at the foot of the

Eiffel Tower, Harris pulled Sofia close. "So, Mrs. Fortune, is Paris everything you hoped it would be?"

"It's everything and more. I never dreamed it would be *this* good."

"Better than the Vegas version?" he teased.

She laughed and glanced at the tower and then lovingly at him. "The real deal is so much better, trust me."

* * * * *

Look for the next installment of the new continuity
The Fortunes of Texas: Fortune's Hidden Treasures

Fortune on His Doorstep
by Michelle Lindo-Rice

On sale November 2025
wherever Harlequin books and ebooks are sold.

And catch up with the previous books

His Family Fortune
by New York Times *bestselling author Elizabeth Bevarly*

Fortune's Fake Marriage Plan
by USA TODAY *bestselling author Tara Taylor Quinn*

Available now!

Get up to 4 Free Books!

We'll send you 2 free books from each series you try
PLUS a free Mystery Gift.

FREE
Value Over
$25

Both the **Harlequin® Special Edition** and **Harlequin® Heartwarming™** series feature compelling novels filled with stories of love and strength where the bonds of friendship, family and community unite.

YES! Please send me 2 FREE novels from the Harlequin Special Edition or Harlequin Heartwarming series and my FREE Gift (gift is worth about $10 retail). After receiving them, if I don't wish to receive any more books, I can return the shipping statement marked "cancel." If I don't cancel, I will receive 6 brand-new Harlequin Special Edition books every month and be billed just $6.39 each in the U.S. or $7.19 each in Canada, or 4 brand-new Harlequin Heartwarming Larger-Print books every month and be billed just $7.19 each in the U.S. or $7.99 each in Canada, a savings of 20% off the cover price. It's quite a bargain! Shipping and handling is just 50¢ per book in the U.S. and $1.25 per book in Canada.* I understand that accepting the 2 free books and gift places me under no obligation to buy anything. I can always return a shipment and cancel at any time by calling the number below. The free books and gift are mine to keep no matter what I decide.

Choose one:
☐ **Harlequin Special Edition**
(235/335 BPA G36Y)

☐ **Harlequin Heartwarming Larger-Print**
(161/361 BPA G36Y)

☐ **Or Try Both!**
(235/335 & 161/361 BPA G36Z)

Name (please print)

Address   Apt. #

City   State/Province   Zip/Postal Code

Email: Please check this box ☐ if you would like to receive newsletters and promotional emails from Harlequin Enterprises ULC and its affiliates. You can unsubscribe anytime.

Mail to the **Harlequin Reader Service:**
IN U.S.A.: P.O. Box 1341, Buffalo, NY 14240-8531
IN CANADA: P.O. Box 603, Fort Erie, Ontario L2A 5X3

Want to explore our other series or interested in ebooks? Visit www.ReaderService.com or call 1-800-873-8635.

*Terms and prices subject to change without notice. Prices do not include sales taxes, which will be charged (if applicable) based on your state or country of residence. Canadian residents will be charged applicable taxes. Offer not valid in Quebec. This offer is limited to one order per household. Books received may not be as shown. Not valid for current subscribers to the Harlequin Special Edition or Harlequin Heartwarming series. All orders subject to approval. Credit or debit balances in a customer's account(s) may be offset by any other outstanding balance owed by or to the customer. Please allow 4 to 6 weeks for delivery. Offer available while quantities last.

Your Privacy—Your information is being collected by Harlequin Enterprises ULC, operating as Harlequin Reader Service. For a complete summary of the information we collect, how we use this information and to whom it is disclosed, please visit our privacy notice located at https://corporate. harlequin.com/privacy-notice. Notice to California Residents – Under California law, you have specific rights to control and access your data. For more information on these rights and how to exercise them, visit https://corporate.harlequin.com/california-privacy. For additional information for residents of other U.S. states that provide their residents with certain rights with respect to personal data, visit https://corporate.harlequin.com/other-state-residents-privacy-rights/.

HSEHW25